ELEANOR

Beastly Lords Book Seven

A Novella

S̸ydney J̸ane B̸aily

cat whisker press
Massachusetts

This book is a work of fiction. Names, characters, places, and incidents either are products of the author's imagination or are used fictitiously. Any resemblance to actual events or locales or persons, living or dead, is entirely coincidental.

Copyright © 2020 Sydney Jane Baily

All rights reserved under International and Pan-American Copyright Conventions.

First published in the anthology *The Midnight Hour: All Hallows' Brides*, October 2019.

No part of this book may be reproduced or transmitted in any form or by any means, electronic or mechanical, including photocopying, recording, or by any information storage and retrieval system without written permission from the publisher, except for the inclusion of brief quotations in a review or article.

ISBN: 978-1-938732-41-6
Published by **cat whisker press**
Imprint of JAMES-YORK PRESS

Cover: **cat whisker studio**
In conjunction with Philip Ré
Book Design: **cat whisker studio**.

DEDICATION

To Marliss Melton

the Eleanor to my Beryl

OTHER WORKS
by
SYDNEY JANE BAILY

THE RARE CONFECTIONERY
Series

The Duchess of Chocolate
The Toffee Heiress
My Lady Marzipan

THE DEFIANT HEARTS
Series

An Improper Situation
An Irresistible Temptation
An Inescapable Attraction
An Inconceivable Deception
An Intriguing Proposition
An Impassioned Redemption

THE BEASTLY LORDS
Series

Lord Despair
Lord Anguish
Lord Vile
Lord Darkness
Lord Misery
Lord Wrath
Eleanor

PRESENTING LADY GUS

A Georgian-Era Novella

ACKNOWLEDGMENTS

My heartfelt gratitude to Kathryn Le Veque for inviting me to write a story inspired by Edgar Allan Poe. And, as always, huge thanks to my mum, Beryl Baily, just for being there.

CHAPTER ONE

1852, Bedfordshire, England

"There is my wild, untamed friend," were the words that welcomed Eleanor Blackwood to Angsley Hall under a dreary, gray sky.

As soon as she stepped out of her coach, the wind whipping at her cloak, she was enveloped by her dearest friend, Beryl, who had recently married a pirate, or so she liked to say.

Since Eleanor knew very well that Captain Philip Carruthers was a perfectly upstanding sea captain, she ignored Beryl's teasing accusations regarding her husband, although it would have been an exciting notion—her friend capturing and marrying a dangerous pirate.

Together, she and Beryl Angsley Carruthers had made up many exciting tales in the five years they'd known each other, growing from gawky girls to polished young women. Perhaps no tale was as good as Beryl's true-life adventure, being kidnapped by Chinese pirates and rescued by her dashing Philip, who then married her.

The captain, himself, was right behind his wife, ready to give Eleanor a hug as soon as Beryl released her.

By happy chance, they were visiting Beryl's parents in the Angsley family home in Bedfordshire. While Eleanor's final destination was her sister Maggie's home, Turvey House, it was barely a couple miles away, and she couldn't pass up the opportunity to visit with her best friend.

Besides, Beryl and Philip were expecting a child, and from Eleanor's experience with her two older sisters, after a woman reached a certain size, she simply wanted to go home and stay there. And home for the Carruthers was hundreds of miles southwest on the coast of Cornwall, where Beryl and her sea captain husband resided in a house on the water's edge. Thus, Eleanor might not see her again for many months, if not a year.

"How was your trip?" Beryl asked. "I cannot believe you came by yourself, all the way from Sheffield."

True, it was a three-day journey from the north, but as the baby of the family and a mature nineteen, Eleanor thought she'd been coddled long enough. *Or stifled*, as she sometimes saw it.

"You went all the way to the Orient," she pointed out to Beryl as they sat in the parlor with tea and lemon cake, the happy parents-to-be seated side by side on the sofa.

"I was with my father and the British Navy," her friend declared. "You've done something I've never done—stayed in a country inn alone."

They all laughed, but, in truth, Eleanor had felt both unsettled her first night traveling and also very grown up, while eating her meal alone at a roadside inn.

The Earl of Lindsey, married to Eleanor's eldest sister, Jenny, had chosen every stopping point and sent her in his luxurious coach with a driver and a footman, both armed. Thus, Eleanor had been as safe as if she were in her family's home in Sheffield.

Both in the carriage and at each inn, she had devoured her favorite Gothic novels. Some, she had read many times, such as Mrs. Shelley's *Frankenstein*, and the Brontes' *Wuthering Heights* and *Jane Eyre*. Others, she was reading for the first time, including *Castle of Otranto* and *Mysteries of Udolpho*, which Jenny had given her for the trip.

Alone in the carriage for hours, with the unnerving tone of the stories filling her head, Eleanor had felt goosebumps each time the wind rattled the windows. And each evening, in a strange bedchamber, she had firmly closed the shutters and the drapes, keeping the bedside lamp lit late into the night, while the notion of dark and drafty castles filled her brain.

"I'm so glad you could stop here before going on to see Maggie," Beryl said.

Eleanor would stay a couple days until Beryl and Philip left, and then carry on to her middle sister's home. Maggie had married Beryl's cousin, John Angsley, the Earl of Cambrey, and was the reason Beryl and Eleanor had first met. Luckily, the Angsley brothers, Beryl's father, Harold, and his older brother, Gideon, the former Earl of Cambrey, had kept their estates—Angsley Hall and Turvey House—so close, making it easy for Eleanor to visit first her best friend and then her sister.

A flash of ginger-orange heralded the arrival of Leo, the captain's cat, which went everywhere with him, including out to sea. Suddenly, it jumped onto the sofa, walked across his lap, using him as a steppingstone to get to Beryl.

"Oof," Philip exclaimed. "Damn cat has pile-drivers for paws. He got me right in the—"

"Philip!" Beryl exclaimed, rolling her eyes before stroking Leo as he wedged himself between husband and wife and settled down into a ball.

"He's beautiful," Eleanor said.

All at once, Beryl turned to her husband of just over a year. "You're being awfully quiet."

"I am the same as always," Philip told her, leaning back, crossing one ankle atop the knee of his other leg. "When you are in the room, there is no need for me to speak."

Both girls stared at him. Eleanor wondered if her friend would take offense. Beryl did tend to chat as much as a magpie, but it was something Eleanor cherished about her. They could talk all day about nothing and everything, and never tire of it.

"*Hm*," Beryl mused, then smiled at him. "Because you are captivated by my beauty whenever you're near me?"

"Precisely," he said, and they shared a lover's glance, which nearly made Eleanor feel as if she were intruding.

Bringing them back to a less romantic subject, she asked, "When are you next going to sea?"

Her friend often went with her husband, who was responsible for taking Beryl's father, Lord Harold Angsley, the queen's ambassador to Spain, across the Channel and through the Straits of Gibraltar. Beryl had promised someday Eleanor could go, too. She probably had to stand in line behind her friend's five younger brothers and sisters, whose voices, even then, Eleanor could hear in various parts of the manor.

"She is not going until *after* this baby arrives," Philip answered. "And that's final."

Apparently, they had battled over this. Eleanor was sorry to have brought it up. She didn't know much about the give-and-take—or downright battles—of married couples. Both her sisters had married happily, although they'd had a few rocks in their paths along the way to matrimonial bliss.

In any case, Eleanor had encountered no gentleman during her first or second Season with whom she was interested in battling or giving her heart. At least, *not* in London. Moreover, she had particularly missed Beryl during the past year. The stifling rigidity of the social events was bad enough, but to go to endless balls, picnics, dinner parties, and the like without her favorite companion had made it worse.

Everyone in her family knew London's Season might not suit the youngest Blackwood sister. Known to her family as a nature lover, Eleanor preferred the outdoors in all types of weather to gleaming tiled floors, and she chose sunlight and moonlight over crystal chandeliers. She could be found sketching or reading at all hours, sitting under a tree, perfectly content.

It had been difficult to get a peaceful moment trying to sketch in Hyde Park or Kensington Gardens with hundreds of Londoners and visitors strolling or riding around her. St. James's Park had been hardly any better. And the smoky, foggy air always seemed to choke her at night.

When Eleanor retired to one of Angsley Hall's guest rooms that evening, a heavy thunderstorm still raged across the landscape on an early autumn wind and refused to let up. Accompanied by lightning and silvery sheets of rain, she sat next to the window overlooking the back terrace and gardens, feeling peaceful.

Bedfordshire was bliss, with so much greenery and the lovely River Great Ouse flowing through both her sister's Turvey House and the Angsley Hall estate. Eleanor had caught fish in it when visiting Maggie in the past, and she hoped to catch more in a few days during her extended stay with her sister and her sister's husband, the Earl of Cambrey.

More importantly, she was also looking forward to being once again in close proximity to the raven-haired Grayson O'Connor, the Turvey House estate manager, who looked more like Eleanor's idea of a pirate than Beryl's captain. Or perhaps Grayson reminded her more of an anguished inhabitant of a dreary castle from one of her beloved Gothic novels. Whatever the case, in her regard, he was beyond anyone she had met in London.

Grayson was born right there on the grounds of Angsley Hall to the Angsleys' seamstress. However, he had lived at Turvey House from the time he was a boy, as a companion to young John Angsley, then the heir and now the Earl of Cambrey. Over the course of one spectacular Season, the earl had fallen desperately in love with Maggie—as most men did—making her his Countess of Cambrey.

How fortunate for Eleanor as that meant she had been introduced to Grayson.

Each and every time she had encountered Grayson, she found she liked him more. His humor was to her liking, as was something about his slightly lopsided smile, which appeared often and was always reflected in his dark eyes. He'd taken her riding and fishing and didn't mind spending hours pointing out birds and plants on the Cambrey estate, around Turvey House.

Then there was his sensual mouth, which she truthfully hadn't noticed until about two years earlier, and now found impossible not to look upon when he spoke.

She sighed. Grayson was certainly not a man to be found in an insipid, stifling ballroom!

At that moment, a flash of lightning split the sky, directing her attention to the fields, where . . . she gasped, a lone horseman rode hell bent toward the very manor in which she was residing.

As the lightning's glow faded, she could barely see more than a dark, four-legged shape coming ever onward, obviously drenched.

Gracious! Who would be out so late and in this weather? And why? A shard of lightning could mean instant death for the rider and the horse.

Standing, she tried to keep her eyes trained on the horseman until he disappeared into the shadows near the stables. She waited a while to see the man emerge but didn't. Perhaps he was still tending his horse, or perhaps he had slipped out of the stables, and, in the pitch darkness, she'd missed his passage.

Despite her room being on the third floor, Eleanor listened intently, thinking to hear the mysterious intruder come into the manor, perhaps seeking sustenance as well as shelter. Surely, the servants would be roused if not Lord and Lady Angsley, Beryl's parents.

All remained eerily silent.

ELEANOR

Eventually, Eleanor climbed into the four-poster bed with its thick, soft mattress and settled in, trying to imagine why someone would come so late and yet not come indoors.

Hopefully, the morning would see all her questions answered.

AT FIRST LIGHT, ELEANOR was up, washing her face at the basin in her room, unbraiding, combing, and re-braiding her brown hair before tucking it up with a few pins. What's more, she needed no help from one of the Angsleys' maids to dress as her buttons were in the front, and her day gown was positively plain.

After all the frippery, frills, and finery of the Season, she was positively gleeful wearing a simple, yellow, cotton gown and only one petticoat, along with her corset and chemise.

She had always been an early riser, smiling to herself thinking how she'd often tugged Beryl out of bed when they were visiting Turvey House together.

Wondering if any of the other Angsleys were up, Eleanor went quietly down the stairs and into the morning room. Breakfast had not yet been laid out, but a serving girl was quick to offer her tea or coffee and whatever she wished to eat before a buffet was set out.

Drats! She'd forgotten to ask for extra milk. Dashing after the girl and down the passageway to the rear of the house, she caught Mr. Stanley the butler coming indoors, his boots damp, shaking water off his coat in the anteroom next to the kitchen door.

They stared at one another for a long moment, and she had the feeling he hadn't wanted to be seen entering.

How strange!

"May I help you, Miss Blackwood?"

"I just asked Mary for tea but forgot to request extra milk."

He nodded. "I assure you, the kitchen staff already knows you enjoy plenty of milk with your tea. It will come out just as you like."

She offered him her thanks, turned away to retrace her steps, then remembered the nighttime horseman. Spinning around, she was faced with an empty hall. The damp butler had disappeared as swiftly as dawn mist. Frowning, she returned to the morning room.

During tea and toast, she was greeted by Leo the cat, then the Angsleys' long-time nanny, Mrs. Wendall, and her charges, who were Beryl's two youngest siblings. Lastly, the three other young siblings arrived before Eleanor vacated the room.

Dashing upstairs to retrieve her cloak, she was determined to have a walk while there was still a little mist hovering over the sodden ground.

When in the country, Eleanor always brought her well-worn leather Wellingtons, as everyone called them for the war hero who designed them. At the back door, she removed her indoor kidskin shoes and slipped on these water-repellent boots with ease before heading out.

Due to the dripping trees and wetness everywhere, she hadn't brought out her sketch pad. Settling her hood over her head, she strode off the terrace and into the rose gardens and the wilder terrain beyond. Everything smelled rainwater fresh, and she breathed deeply as she walked.

Halfway across the field at the back of Angsley Hall, a grouse flew out of the long grass ahead of her, startling her into giving a single shriek. In seconds, it had flown away.

Clapping her hands with amusement and to release the surge of energy caused by her initial alarm, Eleanor continued to walk with her heart beating a little faster. One never knew what one would encounter in a meadow or forest. To her, that was part of the appeal.

After walking at least a mile, she began to circle back toward the manor, hoping by the time she reached the hall, the adults would have arisen, and someone could identify the mysterious horseman she had seen the night before.

Better yet, maybe he would be seated in the morning room, and she could see him for herself.

On the path back to Angsley Hall, she came upon what Beryl and her family called the old granary lodge, a remodeled granary set close to the river where the older servants with nowhere else to go, who could no longer offer service, lived out their years. The year before, Eleanor and Beryl had experienced many a delightful afternoon eating sweet biscuits with Mrs. Latbury, the Angsleys' former cook.

When the cook's legs became too bad to stand at the worktable all day, she had retired to the outskirts of the property. She still managed to create batches of the best baked goods, inviting the girls there for lively discussions and slices of toffee cake.

Was it too early to intrude?

The old mill powered with an enormous waterwheel fed by the River Great Ouse had been replaced by a modern mill in the nearby village. To Eleanor, the whitewashed stone building was cheerful, and the mill stone and surging water threading through the channel under the wheel were rather romantic. It belonged to an era of folks making their own butter and cheese, neither of which the current staff at Angsley Hall or the larger one at Turvey House still did.

She walked around the old lodge, recalling which door led to Mrs. Latbury's two rooms, thinking perhaps she would smell something good cooking. Finding the entrance, a blue painted door, she knocked, again hoping it wasn't too early.

The door snapped open, and an unfamiliar face appeared—an old woman with her face scrunched up and her eyes narrowed as she peered out menacingly.

Eleanor flinched and tried to step back.

"You're early!" the woman stated, grabbing Eleanor by the hand and hauling her inside.

CHAPTER TWO

Eleanor shrieked in alarm, tripping over the threshold, her hood falling back over her shoulders as she did.

"Unhand me," she demanded at once to the crone who'd attacked her.

"What on earth is wrong with you, Phoebe? I only wanted you to come out of the morning damp."

Eleanor hesitated. Phoebe was the next youngest of Beryl's sisters, and it dawned on her the woman was not wearing a threatening expression but trying to see her properly. What's more, she wasn't a scary old hag. She was no more than forty-five, Eleanor guessed.

"I'm sorry," she said more calmly. "I'm not Phoebe Angsley. I'm—"

"Eleanor Blackwood," a male voice interrupted, startling her.

Turning, she found herself staring up at the black-haired Grayson O'Connor and feeling her stomach do a little flip of excitement. He must have entered the granary room directly behind her.

"I've been looking for you," he said, making her take a step back.

ELEANOR

HAVING GONE TO THE main house searching for Eleanor, Grayson was surprised to find his quarry right back where he'd started, after awakening that morning in his mother's home, a crick in his neck from sleeping on a cot.

His heart began to hammer at the unexpected sight. Eleanor's eyes were the first thing he always noticed about her—intelligent, thoughtful, curious eyes. Then her lovely face and her luscious mouth, and then lower to her...

He stopped himself from looking lower. She was Maggie's younger sister, probably too young for the likes of him.

"Let the girl come in and catch her breath," his mother said. "So nice to have your company. First, my boy came last night and then this lovely sprite. Eleanor, is it?"

"Mum, this is John Angsley's youngest sister-in-law, down from Sheffield."

He strode past both of them, feeling as if the room had shrunk in size now that Miss Blackwood's vibrant presence was contained in it.

Although she was no taller than an average woman and slender, as his mother had noticed, something about Eleanor reminded him of a woodland fairy from an etching he'd seen. Perhaps it was her gently pointed chin.

Today, her hair, the color of rich toffee, was in loose braids, and a little haphazardly arranged on her head. Knowing she'd done it herself without much care made him smile.

"Would you like tea?" he offered, checking to make sure the stove was stoked before settling his mother's kettle on to boil.

"No, thank you," Eleanor refused. "I didn't mean to intrude. I was looking for Mrs. Latbury. I must have the wrong door."

His mother glanced at him, then back at Eleanor.

"I'm sorry, dear," she said. "Mrs. Latbury passed away about six months ago."

He watched Eleanor's face pale. She was a tenderhearted thing. At Turvey House, he'd seen her lift a baby bird from the ground before insisting he help her replace it in its nest. Naturally, he'd done her bidding.

"I'm terribly sorry to hear that," Eleanor said, her voice sincere. "She was a very sweet person, especially for a cook." Then she covered her mouth. "Oh, gracious. I shouldn't have said that. What I meant was…," she trailed off.

He was enchanted by her fluster. But then what about Miss Blackwood didn't enchant him?

His mother reached over and patted Eleanor's hand.

"We knew what you meant, dear. Cooks are notoriously tough folk. But as you say, she was a sweet one."

After a moment of silence, Eleanor nodded, then she brightened.

"I've forgotten my manners. You *are* Mrs. O'Connor, of course. We *have* met before, when you were up at the hall, and I do recognize you. I simply wasn't expecting you here."

"Plus, I squint something terrible now," his mother confessed. "I probably resemble a raisin. Will you take tea with us, after all?"

He saw Eleanor hesitate, and her gaze flew to him. His heart seemed to thump as they made eye contact, but he nodded encouragingly. His mother loved company. He came over as often as he could from Turvey House, not even three miles away.

As their estate manager, he lived in his own home on the Cambrey property. He had tried to convince his mother to live with him, even more forcefully after she left her service as seamstress for the Angsleys, but she wouldn't budge from their estate and loved her place at the lodge.

"Yes, tea would be very welcome," Eleanor agreed.

Gray felt a measure of relief. It would make it easier to tell young Miss Blackwood the disturbing news he had brought from Turvey House the night before.

"I was expecting Miss Phoebe for a needlepoint lesson," his mother explained. "Normally, I don't go snatching people off my front step."

Eleanor laughed softly before sitting at the small table in the room that served as kitchen and parlor, with the only other room being his mum's small bedroom.

He liked how Eleanor didn't put on airs. Even with two sisters having married titled gentlemen, both becoming countesses, she remained living in a modest country cottage with her mother, Lady Blackwood, widow of a penniless baron.

Moreover, despite how Eleanor traveled between the country estates of her two brothers-in-law or stayed in one of the earls' townhouses in London, she didn't seem to have changed her unassuming, easygoing nature one whit.

Five years ago, he'd first met a young lady with a love of horses and of the natural world, who had a sweet purity that charmed him. Artless, happy, Eleanor found pleasure in rainbows and butterflies. He remembered wondering how she would fare in London when she came out as a debutante.

As it turned out, the year before, she'd handled it with quiet aplomb. His close friendship with her middle sister's husband, John Angsley, whom he called Cam, meant he'd heard a great deal about how Eleanor had grown bored during the Season and disgruntled in London.

Thankfully, she'd also easily seen through the masquerade of ladies and gentlemen putting on their best face, sometimes a patently false one, to gain ground on the marriage mart.

Sometimes, he had wondered why it mattered to him how she fared in London. Having been tasked by Cam with coming to find her at Angsley Hall, and now seeing her again, however, left him in little doubt of his feelings for her.

He was smitten with Miss Blackwood.

"My mother retired a couple months back as her eyesight was too poor to continue as Lady Angsley's seamstress," Grayson explained to Eleanor before glancing at his mum. "By the way, where *are* your spectacles?"

When she shrugged, he sighed and set the filled teapot on the table, before reaching for three cups. She was always losing her new eyeglasses.

"Do you have any milk?" he asked, recalling how Eleanor liked milky tea.

"Of course," his mother said. "Lift the stone. It was delivered fresh an hour ago."

He lifted a flagstone from the floor to reveal his mother's cold storage and drew out a stoppered jug of milk, knowing the thick cream was on top. If Eleanor hadn't been there, he would have scooped it off with a spoon and devoured it.

"I know what you're thinking, lad," his mother said, and he cringed, hoping she wouldn't tell Eleanor.

Thankfully, she didn't say anymore, but the smirk on Eleanor's face indicated she'd guessed.

"I won't be offended if you want the cream, Mr. O'Connor," she said, then offered him an impish tilt to her head.

"Do you call my boy *mister*?" his mum asked, surprised.

"Mum," he warned her, shaking the jug to blend the cream for all of them, and then pouring some in the bottom of each cup.

"I'm only wondering why she doesn't call you Gray like everyone else."

"Because she's not family," he said. "And she's a lady."

Eleanor laughed, and he felt as if he might be blushing at his own *faux pas*.

"Don't listen to him, Mrs. O'Connor. I am simply a regular miss. My sisters are titled ladies, but none of us by birth."

"I've not met your eldest sister," his mother said, "but Lady Cambrey is certainly diverting and quite the beauty."

"Yes, she is," Eleanor said without a hint of jealousy.

Maggie had handled her London Seasons in absolutely the opposite manner to Eleanor—from all accounts, enjoying every moment of sparkle and dazzle, of dancing and champagne, and the attention of men, especially the Earl of Cambrey, whom she snagged for her own.

"Does she stop by here?" Eleanor asked.

"What, here?" His mother's tone was horrified, and they all laughed at the notion. "Before I retired, when I was up at the hall, Lord and Lady Cambrey would come over to dine with his relations. The Angsleys aren't like other families, they treat all us servants as family, too, and I was invited to meet your sister one evening. I even got to hear her play the piano. Didn't I, Gray?"

"Yes, Mum," he agreed.

"Do you visit your son at Turvey House?" Eleanor asked, and Gray watched his mother's face cloud over as it always did at any mention of the place.

"No," she said simply, then turned in her seat to look at him. "Lad, there are biscuits in the tin. Nothing like Mrs. Latbury's homemade shortbread, I'm afraid, but tasty."

They passed a pleasant few minutes before Eleanor suddenly frowned at him.

"I only just recalled, you said you were looking for me. Is that right?"

He paused.

"Yes, I rode over here late last night—"

"I saw you," she interrupted, "from my bedroom window. You were the horseman in the storm."

The thought of her in her bed caused a tightening in his loins. For a moment, he said nothing more.

"I lost sight of your horse by the stables," she added. "It was either very brave or very foolish of you to ride in such weather."

"Most likely foolish," muttered his mother, but he knew she said it lovingly.

Eleanor stared at him, her brown eyes seemingly richer and darker than he recalled.

"You came here to see me?" she asked.

He had to tell her, wishing it wasn't going to upset her while knowing with certainty it would.

"I came here to warn you. You must not—nay, you are forbidden—to go to Turvey House."

CHAPTER THREE

Eleanor gasped. She'd been staring at Grayson's mouth as usual, watching his attractive lips form words, wondering what it would feel like to be kissed by him. She'd been kissed during her debutante Season by a rascal who waylaid her behind a copse of trees in Kensington Gardens in broad daylight after a picnic. Her mother had been distracted for only a moment. That was all it took.

She was initially horrified but then, out of sheer curiosity, didn't push away the young man. It was her first kiss, and Eleanor had truly wanted to see what all the fuss was about.

Apparently, nothing at all, was her conclusion.

Still, other girls said a kiss could make one's head spin and ones' feet lift off the ground. Others said it caused one's heart to race. Moreover, she'd read for herself about other more wondrous changes to the body that could happen upon being overly excited by a man.

All she'd felt was a crumb from the rascal's sandwich brush off his lip onto hers, followed quickly by a strong upheaval of revulsion. She'd thought she might lose her delicious picnic lunch. Then he'd walked away, whistling happily as if he'd conquered an army.

Gray's words penetrated her recollections.

"Whatever do you mean, warn me? I'm going to Turvey House tomorrow. I've come all this way."

"You cannot," he said, his tone firm.

"What's the matter at Turvey?" his mother asked.

Gray glanced from her to his mother, and a shiver of fear ran through Eleanor.

Finally, he said, "It's Margaret. She has a slight fever."

Eleanor stood up. "I must go to her at once."

"No, that's why Cam sent me. They don't want to take a chance on her having something contagious."

"That's absurd. I'm her sister. I must go tend to her."

"Don't be selfish," he snapped.

"Gray!" his mother admonished him.

"How can you say that?" Eleanor asked him.

He'd never said a cross word to her before, except warning her once to duck when she rode under a low branch ahead of him.

"I say that because I don't want Margaret to have to worry about you. She has their little one, Rosie, to think of, and she doesn't want Cam to fall ill. And she needs to focus on feeling better and not worrying whether you are going to get sick, too."

Eleanor paused, and then looked at Mrs. O'Connor, who nodded her agreement. She sagged back into the chair.

"Is she very sick?"

"No, not terribly. A little warm, a little light-headed."

"Sometimes, the change of seasons will do that to a person," Grayson's mother pointed out.

Eleanor nodded, then she recalled her plans.

"Beryl and Philip are leaving tomorrow. I can hardly impose on Lord and Lady Angsley after they leave. I am supposed to look after Rosie for a month. What if I stay out of Maggie's room except for standing in the doorway?"

Grayson shook his head. "We all know the Angsleys. You will not be viewed as an imposition if you stay here for a little while longer. Maybe Margaret will feel better soon, or, if Rosie shows no signs, perhaps she can come here. All I know is Cam will have my hide if I allow you to show up at Turvey. You know how he is. He dotes on your sister and is already frightened."

She wanted to weep. If Cam was worried, there was probably reason to be.

"Now you've frightened her," Mrs. O'Connor said to her son. Then she reached out and patted Eleanor's hand.

"Finish your tea and then go tell them up at the hall what's happened. They'll be thrilled to have you stay longer, my dear. Don't you worry. And my Gray will keep you entertained."

Eleanor considered what that meant exactly. *Was he staying at Angsley, too?*

"Mother, I have to—" he began.

"Don't you gainsay me, lad. If Miss Eleanor had made it to Turvey House, you would've kept her company, taking her riding and such. A little chess in the evening, too, I imagine. You can do those things here as easily. They'll give you a room up at the manor."

Those were the normal things Eleanor had done with Grayson in years prior, along with fishing, charades, and cards, but they'd almost always been in a group.

More than a little embarrassed at being foisted upon him, she stood again, just as there was a knock at the door.

"That'll be Miss Phoebe," Mrs. O'Connor said as Grayson also stood.

"I'll let her in." Eleanor reached the door. "Thank you for the information about my sister," she said to Grayson. "But I don't need a nursemaid or a court jester to entertain me. I have my books and my sketchpad, and I'll write letters to my sisters and my mother."

"Court jester?" Grayson muttered under his breath.

Eleanor smiled at his mother. "It was nice to see you, Mrs. O'Connor." Then, she let in a surprised Phoebe.

"Beryl is looking for you," the girl said as she slipped past.

Eleanor strode across the paving stones in front of the old granary lodge.

And all she had wanted was a sweet biscuit!

With her sister fallen sick, everything had gone wrong in an instant. She could still slip away, thwart Grayson, and go to Turvey House, but he was very close friends with Maggie's husband, the Earl of Cambrey. Like brothers. She did not want the earl to blame Grayson for her disobedience.

Moreover, if John didn't want her there, he would be angry to see her, and she didn't like to think of a furious brother-in-law.

At least the mystery was solved. The shadowy horseman, so fanciful and romantic the night before, had turned out to be Grayson come to ruin her entire trip. She had the irrational urge to weep.

"Eleanor," came his voice, just when her feet left the pavers and hit the damp grass again. "I'll go to the hall and explain. I was already there this morning, not expecting you up and out so early."

She shrugged. *What could she say?* She was an oddity, always up early.

"I should have remembered," he added. "You are awake with the birds."

Why should he have recalled such a thing?

"Where did you sleep last night?" she asked when he fell into step beside her. "In the stables?"

"No, this court jester had a cot," he told her. "I pulled it out from under my mother's bed and slept in her front room by the stove. I do it as often as I can get over here to see her."

He rubbed his lower back. "Honestly, a pile of hay in the stables would probably be more comfortable."

She imagined his tall form curled on a narrow cot and nearly laughed. Then she remembered he had inconvenienced himself for her.

"Thank you for coming to tell me. I'm sorry I called you a jester. You have always been good company, even when Beryl and I were pushed onto you along with all her siblings to give the earl time alone with my sister."

He offered her his lopsided smile, which she adored. "Oh, you realized that, did you?"

She sighed. She was not a child any longer.

As they approached the back lawn, two of the Angsleys' dogs came rushing across it to greet them.

"Good dogs," Grayson said, reaching down to pat the spaniels. After a moment, the dogs scented something and tore off into the wooded area at the edge of the property.

Eleanor recalled the grouse from earlier and hoped it was far away from these hunting dogs. She knew their job was to flush out birds from the bushes and tall grass. At that moment, though, floppy and playful, with their tongues lolling out of their mouths, they didn't seem harmful at all.

"Eleanor!" Beryl was standing on the terrace amongst potted plants and the outdoor dining furniture.

Eleanor waved to her.

"You speak with Beryl," Grayson suggested. "I'll go talk to Lord and Lady Angsley."

Eleanor would have liked to make sure her hosts weren't being pressed to allow her an extended visit, but she nodded.

He strode on ahead, gave Beryl a quick hug as he passed, for they'd grown up practically as cousins, and then disappeared through the back entrance.

"What's going on?" Beryl asked as Eleanor gained the terrace. "Why is Gray here?"

"Maggie is sick, and I've been forbidden to go to Turvey until she's well."

Beryl exclaimed in dismay. "I'm so sorry." She enveloped her in a hug, but they were kept slightly apart by the burgeoning baby in her stomach. "Philip and I can put off our journey home."

Eleanor's heart soared momentarily, then she recalled Grayson's unkind word—*selfish*.

"No, that's not necessary. You have far to go, and the longer you wait, the harder it will be on you. Besides, I have all your siblings to keep me company."

They laughed, knowing what troublemakers the younger Angsleys could be.

"And Gray," Beryl reminded her with a pointed look and an arched eyebrow.

When she was sixteen, Eleanor had shared her infatuation over the Turvey House estate manager, and Beryl had never forgotten.

Her cheeks warmed.

"Is he staying?" her best friend asked.

"I'm not certain," Eleanor told her. "His mother thinks he should."

"He should!" agreed Beryl. "You can have loads of fun. The sun will come out eventually so you can do things outdoors. And in the evenings, he'll play cards and chess."

"Honestly, you sound like Mrs. O'Connor. I don't need the sun to be happy, nor a playmate to keep myself occupied."

THAT NIGHT WAS ANOTHER rainy one, keeping everyone indoors. After a brief recital of piano music by Beryl and Phoebe, the drawing room was filled with young and old, playing games. Eleanor's mind kept drifting to Maggie, hoping her sister was already beginning to feel better. She had penned a letter to her after lunch, sending it to Turvey House via the Angsleys' footman, as Beryl thought it best not to let Grayson leave in case he didn't return.

When she told Eleanor that, her cheeks infused with color.

Mortifying! If Grayson wanted to leave, he should go. After all, he could stay in his own home on the Cambrey estate without threat of catching anything from Maggie.

However, that night, he showed no discontentment at being in the company of Eleanor, the Angsleys, and the Carruthers. He'd grown up not as a servant or even as a servant's son, but simply as a companion to John Angsley, the only heir to the earldom. And these were John's relations, uncle, aunt, and cousins, and thus, they seemed to be Grayson's relations, too.

Oddly, no one whom Eleanor had previously asked, not Beryl, Maggie, or John, knew anything about Grayson's father. Moreover, Maggie's husband had said Grayson, himself, didn't know anything more than his father had been a servant who'd died.

After growing up at Turvey House with the old earl and countess and John, Grayson then went to a local boarding school before taking over the position as estate manager. At some point, he had been given land and, thus, built a house near the river.

Over a pot of gossip-water, Maggie had once told Eleanor how Grayson also made money in stocks and occasionally went to London for entertainment.

When pressed, her sister said he'd never brought a woman back to Turvey House, not while she'd been there. Nor did Maggie think he had ever given his heart away to anyone.

Grayson was thus a mystery. *So attractive and smart, why hadn't he yet found a wife?*

Of course, in London, or even here in Bedfordshire, it was entirely possible he had female company on a regular basis. That could be his primary reason for going to London.

Eleanor was quite sure he never grabbed a woman behind a tree and hastily kissed her while leaving food on her face.

She couldn't help watching him. He moved so easily from being down on the floor with the youngest Angsleys, playing checkers and even her old favorite game, *Puss, Puss in the Corner*, to playing cards with the adults. Just as effortlessly, he moved between the worlds of working for John and Maggie as their estate manager to being John's best friend, she supposed.

When the children had gone to bed, except young Asher Angsley, who doted on Captain Philip and sat at his feet, the rest of them decided on charades. Grayson chose Eleanor for his partner, which delighted her. Moreover, as it turned out, they were quite good at communicating and won two rounds.

After that, someone suggested they each propose a riddle. Beryl groaned.

"Why are you moaning?" Eleanor asked her friend. "This is the best part of the evening."

"Only because you love riddles and can guess them nearly every time, while I am utterly hopeless at them."

Eleanor laughed, but it was true. After Beryl's father, Lord Harold Angsley, started them off with more of a pun than a riddle, he said guests should go next and looked to her to offer one.

She scooted forward on the sofa. "Do you know the one that starts like this?

I sit on a rock whilst I'm raising the wind,
But, the storm once abated, I'm gentle and kind;
I've kings at my feet who await but a nod,
To kneel in the dust on the ground I have trod."

Beryl groaned again, causing Leo to lift his furry orange head from the sofa and gaze quizzically at his mistress.

"That's utter nonsense," she muttered.

Philip put an arm around her shoulders to soothe his crotchety, child-carrying wife.

Eleanor looked around. "Has anyone heard it before? If not, there is more to it, and I should be happy to recite it all."

Grayson sat back with a thoughtful look on his handsome face, nearly distracting her into forgetting the riddle's solution. Then he folded his arms over his chest.

"Go on," he prompted her. "We're listening."

She recited the next eight lines, ending with "And when I'm discovered, you'll say with a smile that my first and my last are the pride of this isle."

Lady Catherine Angsley, Beryl's mother, frowned and made her repeat it twice more. Then she proclaimed, "I believe my daughter is correct. It is nonsense."

"It has an answer," Eleanor promised her. "And when you hear it, the hints and clues all make sense. Do you all give up?"

"No, I don't, and I shall wager Philip doesn't either," Grayson said.

"Nor do I," said Lord Angsley. "What's more, I'll wager my wife and I can come up with the answer before Grayson and Philip."

"Oh, dear!" exclaimed Lady Angsley. "Are you certain you wish to partner with me?"

"It's either you or Beryl," his lordship said, causing his daughter to toss a velvet cushion at his head.

After reciting it again, Eleanor waited, delighted to have stumped them all on her first try. However, after a few minutes of conferring with his partner, Grayson lifted his head and smiled.

"I think we've got it. As long as Philip confirms what the pride of the British Isles is."

"The Royal Navy, of course."

"Then the answer," said Grayson, "is a raven."

"Bravo," Eleanor said. "Isn't this fun?"

"No!" said Beryl. After a few more minutes, she declared herself too tired to keep her eyes open, and she and Philip went to bed, taking their cat with them.

This left Eleanor and Grayson with Lord and Lady Angsley. For the second night, there was lightning and thunder, and Eleanor was glad not to be at alone at an inn.

"I'm very pleased not to be travelling on a night like this," she said.

Lord Angsley, who loved to travel, began an interesting story about his recent trip to Spain on the queen's business.

Suddenly, pounding at the front door reverberated through the lofty foyer and sounded loudly in the drawing room.

Lady Angsley gasped, while Eleanor and Grayson jumped to their feet.

CHAPTER FOUR

"Settle down, everyone," Lord Angsley commanded. "Mr. Stanley will see the person in."

In a moment, the lanky butler appeared in the drawing room doorway.

"Who was it?" his lordship demanded.

"Messenger from Turvey House, my lord."

"Show him in at once," said Lady Angsley.

"He has left already, my lady." Whipping an envelope from behind his back, Mr. Stanley handed the damp missive to his lordship. "He brought this for you or for Mr. O'Connor."

"He ought to spend the night," Grayson said.

"He is, sir. In the stables."

The butler turned and left as the house was rattled by another large boom of thunder. Somewhere abovestairs, one of the children shrieked with glee as much as fear.

Lord Angsley raised his eyes to the ceiling. "I should have asked for brandy. Perfect thing on a night like tonight. Dratted man disappears so quickly."

"What does it say, dear?" his wife urged him.

Eleanor felt like snatching it from his lordship's hands since it might have to do with Maggie, but he opened the note, shook it, held it up, read it, and reread it.

"For God's sake," Grayson said, because he had that level of familial relationship with this family, he could express his frustration. "What does it say, my lord?"

"Basically, not to let you go back to Turvey House, either. Now, my nephew is feeling unwell, too."

"Oh dear," her ladyship exclaimed, immediately pulling the bell pull. "We do need brandy."

"Is John very sick?" Eleanor asked.

"He says only that he feels ill. Nothing more. He says to watch you for signs, too." Lord Angsley looked at Grayson. "If you've brought any fever to this house, young man, I shall not look kindly upon it."

Grayson nodded. "I feel fine. Moreover, I was in London up until a day ago. Just when I got back, I was sent here. I had no contact with Lady Cambrey whatsoever."

It still sounded strange to Eleanor's ears for her sister to be called by her title.

"Good," his lordship said.

Mr. Stanley reappeared, and soon the brandy tray arrived.

"And what of John's mother?" Lady Angsley asked.

Eleanor was fond of the other Lady Cambrey, the dowager. She was a kind mother-in-law to Maggie.

"In London, at present," Grayson said. "I escorted her there myself a couple weeks ago."

"Good," his lordship repeated himself. "Less people to worry about."

They sat in silence for a while, all four sipping brandy and listening to the rain drum against the windows.

"You were in London recently, weren't you?" Lady Angsley asked Eleanor.

"Yes, I was. For the entire Season." She tried not to sound fed up by the entire tedious ordeal.

"We were there for the opening race at Ascot and, of course, for the Derby." Lady Angsley looked to her husband for confirmation.

"I was at the Derby," Eleanor said. "I'm sorry I didn't see you there. Except for that delightful day in Surrey, I believe I spent the majority of my time in stuffy ballrooms and dining rooms in Town."

Her ladyship sent her a questioning smile. "And you didn't find your ideal suitor?"

Eleanor felt her cheeks grow warm. It was a rather personal question but seeing as she'd been in and out of the Angsleys' house for five years, she supposed it was all right for Lady Angsley to ask.

Yet Grayson seemed to be listening intently, too, and she hated to sound like a failure.

"I met some interesting gentlemen," she said, thinking of the few men she could actually recall and how interestingly vain, boring, or dull they were.

Lady Angsley turned to Grayson. "You were here last night?"

He seemed to still be considering her answer, for he paused before he answered. "Yes, I stayed at the granary lodge with my mother."

"I miss having her in the house," her ladyship said. "I'm so glad Phoebe—"

A gun shot rendered the night, interrupting her.

"HELL'S BELLS!" LORD ANGSLEY exclaimed. "What next? Armageddon and pestilence?"

Gray jumped to his feet again and headed for the door.

"Everyone, stay here," he ordered, belatedly realizing he didn't have the right to order anyone to do anything but hoped they would listen anyway.

Footsteps on the main stairs heralded the arrival of Captain Carruthers rushing down to his side, only half-dressed but armed.

As a privateer—some said pirate—Beryl's husband probably always slept with one eye open and a gun in his hand. Gray didn't know him too well, except as the man who'd saved Beryl's life more than once, for which he was grateful, as she was like a sister to him.

"It could be nothing," Gray told him, then a shot rang out again. "Or maybe something," he added, grabbing a cloak from the front hall cupboard. He tossed one to Philip, as Mr. Stanley reappeared.

"We'll check this out. Maybe those in the drawing room need more brandy."

"Yes, sir."

With the captain by his side, Gray dashed out into the night, his second encounter with a nasty thunderstorm in two days. He didn't need to worry about catching Maggie's fever. He would probably get chilblains or be struck by lightning first.

Philip paused beside him on the gravel at the front of the house. "I hate to say this, but unless there are more shots, we can't possibly determine where the first ones came from."

In answer, there was a third shot, clearly ringing out from behind the house.

"That's fortunate, then, isn't it?" Gray quipped, and they took off at a run into the darkness around the side of the house.

With heavy rain pelting him, stinging his face, he circled one side of the manor while the captain went around the other way. The lightning, which had been blocked by the heavy curtains in the drawing room, flashed stark and white across the sky every few moments, and the thunderclouds boomed close by.

They reached the terrace simultaneously, then headed into the gardens, and finally onto the back lawn. All was quiet.

Suddenly, he heard barking, recalling the spaniels who'd dashed off toward the trees that morning.

In the brilliant, blinding flash of the next lightning bolt, he spied one of them running hell bent toward him, something in its mouth.

As it approached, Gray could see the dog had a chicken. A moment or two later, the other one appeared, and for a moment, he imagined it had been shot because of something sticky plastering its soft fur, but it was running too well.

"Drop it," he ordered the dog, and to his surprise, the dog released the dead bird. Obviously, it was well-trained for hunting. The other dog, however, scooped it up and took off toward the house with its littermate in pursuit. Gray couldn't tell if it was covered in mud or blood.

"I'll get ye," came a voice out of the darkness, along with the familiar sound of a shotgun barrel being snapped back into place after reloading.

"Sir," Philip called out, "you are on Angsley land. Lower your weapon."

"What?" came the man's voice. And another flash of lightning showed he'd turned toward them, gun haphazardly pointed in their direction.

"Lower your gun," Gray repeated the captain's command.

"Or I'll shoot you where you stand," Philip added, sounding as piratical as Beryl said he was.

"Oy, some foxes have been at me chickens," the man said, but he did as told and lowered his shotgun.

"Not foxes, sir," Gray explained. "His lordship's hunting spaniels."

"What ye say?"

"It's true," Gray added. "We just saw them with one of your chickens. Your name, sir?"

"McNeil. My place is just past the grove, about two furlongs to the west. Spaniels, you say?"

"Yes. Come back tomorrow," Gray instructed him, "and you'll be compensated for your chicken."

"More than one," he said. "They dropped the other one. That's two chickens." He held up his hand, two fingers pointed to the sky.

Philip muttered something under his breath about counting chickens.

"Tomorrow, then," Gray reminded the man. "And don't fire your weapon on Angsley land again. You could have hurt someone."

"Bah!" grunted the man whose name Gray recognized as a local farmer. "Blasted dogs." And he wandered off.

They watched him take a few steps, and then they turned and started back to the house.

"Stuff like that doesn't happen on board ship," Philip pointed out. "Far more peaceful on the high seas."

Gray laughed. They went inside through the servant's door, finding the dogs had got there ahead of them. The spaniels, filthy and still fighting over the poor cockerel, were contained in the mudroom. When informed a stable hand had been called to take the dogs away and clean them, Gray and Philip removed their muddy shoes and damp cloaks and headed in their stockinged feet for the parlor.

"Just an angry farmer," Gray explained to the waiting group, despite being unable to look away from Eleanor's big, brown eyes.

"I bid you all goodnight again," the captain said, saluting with his pistol before disappearing upstairs once more.

"A good man to have at one's side," Gray said, taking a seat next to Eleanor. "Did I miss anything exciting in here?"

"We were discussing literature," Eleanor said, and he realized he was relieved he'd been outside in the pouring rain. The deluge was preferable to the silly romantic serials in the paper that women usually discussed, none of which he'd read or had an interest in reading.

On the other hand, Beryl liked a wide variety of texts. Maybe Eleanor was the same.

"What do you like to read, Miss Eleanor?" he asked.

"Gothic literature," she declared, surprising him. "Anything dark and exciting. Rather the way it has been around here since I arrived."

"What?" his lordship exclaimed. "Angsley Hall, dark and exciting?"

Eleanor laughed, a sound Gray had enjoyed many times over the years.

"Truly, my lord. Ever since I arrived, there have been heavy clouds, thunder, rain, and lightning."

"Like every other part of Britain, most of the time," Lord Angsley said. "I don't think there's anything particularly Gothic about it. But for better weather, you must come with me some time to Spain. When I have my next commission, perhaps. If Beryl is going, you can provide company."

"I don't believe she'll be going until after she has been delivered of her little one," her ladyship informed her husband.

"In any case, it's not merely the weather," Eleanor said. "It's the clever way the writer includes terrifying nature in the story."

"Terrifying nature," Gray repeated, watching her pretty lips with their hint of pink, along with her healthy cheeks. *Or was she wearing artful cosmetics?*

"Yes, as if it were a character, like the storm in Mary Shelley's masterful book. And sometimes the writer assigns human intelligence to things in the natural world."

"Such as?" he prompted.

"The whale in Moby Dick," she offered.

"Or Mr. Poe's Raven," he added, thoroughly enjoying their conversation.

"The American writer," she said. "I've never read him. I hear he's excellent. In any case, when you combine all that with mysterious circumstances, it transforms the ordinary into the Gothic. It's really all in how one perceives the situation, sometimes not knowing the reality. Do you see what I mean?"

His lordship frowned, and her ladyship yawned. Gray felt badly for Eleanor, who was trying so hard to explain.

"You mean like the gunfire," he suggested, "that turned out to be only a farmer but could have been a madman coming to do us all in?"

The Angsleys both exclaimed aloud, but Eleanor grinned.

"Precisely," she said, turning back to Lord Angsley. "And then there was the mysterious night rider, which turned out to be Mr. O'Connor arriving last night—"

"Please, feel free to call me Grayson."

"Very well."

They locked gazes for an instant too long. A man could get lost in those gorgeous eyes. *If that man didn't think of her as a little cousin!*

"As I was saying, when Grayson arrived so late, like a knight charging across the field to his castle, it was straight out of a Gothic tale."

"Absurd," Lord Angsley said.

"Or even the butler bursting in with a missive," Eleanor pointed out.

"Mr. Stanley doesn't burst," Lady Angsley protested.

"Still," Eleanor continued, "do you see how those few easily explained circumstances, when combined with a dark night and a storm, can set a certain tone? That's Gothic literature. Most thrilling! Especially when one is safely tucked in bed or in a cozy chair by the fire, and the damsel on the damp moors or the man kept in chains in his castle is only on the pages."

"I see what you mean, dear," Lady Angsley said as she stood, causing both men to rise with her. "I prefer a plain novel of manners, with no hint of nerve-wracking elements. Simply men and women going about their lives, like one of Jane Austen's works, God rest her soul. Such a talent!"

Gray and Eleanor bid the lord and lady goodnight, and then they sat back down. He was immediately aware they were unusually and rather unacceptably alone.

"Are you thinking what I am?" he asked.

"That one of us is supposed to tell the other he or she is retiring, whether we want to or not, simply because if a member of polite society—"

"Or even impolite society, like the *ton*," he pointed out.

"Yes, or even impolite society wandered in, then we should be considered scandalous. You might even be forced to marry me."

"Egad! Forced to marry a lovely lass? What a horror!" He leaned back on the sofa, letting his head drop back slightly and stretching out his legs. "I missed out on the second glass of brandy, and I intend yet to enjoy it. I would be pleased if you would keep me company, and I will grab farmer McNeil's shotgun and let loose upon the first member of the *ton* I see peering through the window."

He was rewarded with her heartfelt laugh. She didn't cover her mouth. She simply chuckled freely, and her entire body moved with mirth.

"Well," he said.

She paused, regarding him. "Well, what?"

"My brandy, woman. Where is it?"

Playing along, she went to the sideboard and poured them each another fingerful into glasses she chose from the tray.

"That might not have been your original glass," she confessed, handing it to him and letting her fingers graze his.

He could grab her hand and pull her onto his lap and kiss her.

Christ, man! Get a grip! She was Maggie's younger sister, after all. And he was thinking like a besotted twit. This was the same girl he'd taken fishing, surprised when she could bait a hook without help, even more surprised when she could haul in a fish with dexterity. He'd hunted with her although she declined to shoot anything live and only did target practice with his hunting rifle. They'd ridden together on more than one occasion, and she'd helped him teach the younger Angsley children to sit upon a saddle some mornings when they were all staying at Turvey, while Beryl was still in bed.

"You are quiet, Grayson," she murmured.

He realized he'd been staring at her, swirling the brandy in his glass. To her credit, she hadn't asked him what was on his mind or started up an inane conversation. She had simply let him be. He liked that tremendously about her.

But then, what about her didn't he like?

"I was only thinking…"

"Yes?" she prompted after a long moment's silence.

"How wonderful you are." He couldn't help smiling after he'd said what was in his heart. *At last!*

Her eyes grew so wide, he assumed he'd shocked her. Until she blinked.

Then she returned his smile. He saw her draw a deep breath, knew it by how the curves of her breasts rose and fell. Then with a tilt of her lovely head, she charmed him.

"That is very strange," she began, "because I was thinking the same thing about you."

CHAPTER FIVE

Eleanor decided she might as well be honest. However, as soon as she said the words, Grayson frowned. Then he downed the last of his drink and stood.

"I shouldn't have said what I said. I definitely shouldn't have been so forward," he added, "especially not when we are alone."

"We could hardly speak that way if we weren't alone," she pointed out.

"True, which is why we shouldn't have been alone in the first place. You're Maggie's little sister."

"And what of it?" she asked, gulping back the last of her brandy, letting it create a warm trail down the back of her throat before coming to her feet.

Immediately, Eleanor realized she was standing a little too close to him, but if she stepped back now, it would seem as if she weren't at ease. And downing her brandy so quickly had made her decidedly care-free.

It seemed being in the country allowed for different rules. She'd discussed this very fact with Beryl in the past but never put the notion into practice. Until now.

Eleanor stepped even closer, and Grayson had nowhere to go, as his shapely calves were pressed against the sofa. He seemed to be under the mistaken belief she was too young for him.

A ridiculous thought! He didn't have a single wrinkle or gray hair. What's more, he was the most virile, attractive man she knew.

"Eleanor," he warned. "What are you doing?"

What was she doing?

"I'm leaning in so you can kiss me. Only if you wish, of course," she added, not wanting to be deemed pushy.

He said nothing, looking into her eyes, then his gaze dropped to her lips, and a thrill of excitement sizzled through her. He was considering it, she could tell.

After a pause, during which she wondered if she looked ridiculous waiting for him, her lips slightly parted, she began to feel anxious.

Should she grab hold of him or wrap her arms around his neck?

Before she could fathom what to do next, he asked, "Have you been kissed before?"

Thank goodness she could answer truthfully. If she'd had to say no, she would have sounded like the greenest ninny who ever reached the age of nineteen.

"Yes, naturally. After all, I've had a couple Seasons in London." Eleanor tossed her head, making her curls flow over her shoulder as she'd seen Maggie do.

Grayson fell silent again, still considering.

"And did you find a young spark who caught your fancy this Season?"

They were all boys compared to the man who stood before her.

"No," she admitted.

He smiled and shook his head. "You were supposed to say yes and try to make me jealous. That's how the game is played."

"Is it? How silly of me not to know that." She was the one staring at his lips now, knowing if he kissed her, it would be very good. However, apparently, she wasn't playing the game of flirtation correctly.

Eleanor sighed, wishing he would simply—

His large hands suddenly clasped her shoulders and held her still. She gasped softly, looking up at him again, just as he lowered his head, and placed his mouth upon hers.

Her first thought was *brandy*, followed quickly by a far more impossibly wonderful one: *Grayson O'Connor was kissing her!*

Then, she couldn't think at all, as he tilted his head and seemed to fit his mouth to hers even more tightly. She felt hot all over and even a little light-headed. Maybe Maggie wasn't sick. Maybe she'd simply been kissing John too much.

When she heard—and felt—him groan against her lips, it caused her heartbeat to speed up even more. Eleanor realized she'd taken hold of his lightweight jacket and was scrunching his lapels with her fingers.

Then he opened his mouth against hers and, as the intensity of their kiss deepened, the sizzling sensations of desire trickled through her body like heated brandy. Mimicking him, she parted her lips beneath his.

His hands slipped from her shoulders to stroke down her back and rest just above the swell of her moderate bustle. To her amazement, he drew her in tightly against his body, and she could feel the strength of him from chest to hips and down his long muscular thighs.

Deep inside her own body, she tingled, and without meaning to, without thinking about it, she tilted her hips against him.

And then it was over. Grayson released her suddenly, letting her go so quickly, she had to keep her grasp on his coat or risk falling over. But in a moment, he had hold of her hands and was prying them loose and pushing her away.

"I'm sorry," were his first words.

Not lover's words, not anything she wanted to hear.

"Whyever for?"

He ran a hand distractedly through his coal-black hair. "I was wrong to kiss you."

Again, she asked, "Why? I didn't protest, and I liked it."

"You're young. A debutante."

She laughed. "I'm not a debutante, and I haven't been since last year. Besides, that signifies nothing. I could have come out a year earlier and have had my third London Season, or I could have had an overly protective mother and been kept at home entirely."

Grayson stared at her, then seemed to realize, despite the distance between them, he was still holding her hands.

"You're Maggie's little sister," he muttered and dropped his hold.

Eleanor rolled her eyes, suddenly tired from the many ups and downs of the day, particularly this last emotional seesaw. She wanted to lie quietly in the big, soft bed Lady Angsley had given her and recall every scrumptious moment of the kiss.

Rot it all! She'd meant to touch his hair, so soft looking. If he decided never to kiss her again, she would have lost her chance.

Slowly, she reached her fingers toward his hair.

He froze, his eyes swiveling to watch her movements, until her hand disappeared behind his head, and then his gaze locked on hers.

"What are you doing?" his voice was a shocked whisper.

"I've wanted to touch your hair for a long time," she confessed. "So pretty, like a raven's wing." And then she sunk her fingertips into the hair at the nape of his neck. She watched him close his eyes, looking almost pained.

"I suppose you'll tell me I shouldn't," she said, stroking her fingers through its soft thickness. "After all, you're old enough to be my father."

His eyes popped open. "Hardly that. Not even possible."

She started to laugh, and he stopped talking, knowing he'd been baited.

ELEANOR

Drawing back, Eleanor walked deliberately and casually to the drawing room door before giving him a last glance. She might not know much about flirtation, but she did know it was better to leave while she was ahead and not to overstay her welcome.

Let him think about her and their kiss and how silly it was to worry about her age as she was obviously a fully-grown woman—one whose knees happened to be trembling as she left the room.

SINCE HIS GUEST ROOM was on the same floor as hers, although at the other end of a long, wide hallway, Gray waited a few minutes after Eleanor left before going upstairs.

He didn't fall easily asleep. He had kissed Eleanor Blackwood, and he'd thoroughly enjoyed it, except for the sense of guilt directly afterward.

Maggie's younger sister. Beryl's best friend. A baron's daughter, not a servant's offspring. *Did those things matter?*

If he were honest, it was the best first kiss he'd ever had, better than the first with any new lady-friend. His body had leaped to attention, and he'd felt his heart thumping in his chest.

He hadn't even touched her tongue with his, but he'd certainly wanted to. At the same time, he would have liked to cup her full breasts and grind himself against her. Somehow, he'd refrained, only by holding himself still and focusing on the feel of her soft lips under his.

If she'd been any other willing woman, he would have done much more, probably ending up with her splayed beneath him on the Angsleys' sofa. But this was Eleanor. Clearly not a child anymore, yet still he had the need to protect her and care for her, the way he did for Beryl or the other young Angsleys.

On top of that, however, was the avid desire to explore every inch of her. *How could he be so torn between wanting to cherish her and to make love to her until she couldn't walk?*

Lying in bed, one arm thrown over his eyes, Grayson groaned as he had done into her mouth, recalling what a pleasure it had been to finally kiss her. One time, a year prior, she'd winked at him over the breakfast table at Turvey House, and he'd been rocked to his core by how alluring that small gesture had seemed.

Eleanor was accomplished, good fun, and rather splendid. Moreover, when he was in the company of other females, he couldn't help comparing them and finding them lacking. London was a necessity for his business dealings, whether handling some order for the Cambrey estate or meeting with his broker to trade on the London Stock Exchange.

And when he went every few months, he usually sought out the same couple of ladies. Neither Cyprians, nor eligible ladies, they were simply women who didn't mind spending an evening dining, talking, and copulating. One was a widow about five years his senior, and one was a confirmed bluestocking and spinster, who vowed she would never let a man own her through marriage.

Neither knew about the other, and, thus, his need for female company was taken care of. Rather nicely, too. But he was starting to want more.

First, he'd seen Cam's best friend, Simon Devere, marry Jenny Blackwood, Eleanor's oldest sister, after knowing her a very short while, and then Cam, himself, had fallen prey to the swaying bustle and dazzling smile of Maggie, the middle Blackwood sister.

As for himself, a few years back, he hadn't given Eleanor a second thought or glance, but she'd barely been out of childhood, or so he'd told himself, even when it was obvious she had curves to spare and the sharp mind of a woman.

With each visit to Turvey House, she became dearer to him, and as each year passed, she changed from awkward teenager into a young woman. Not polished like Maggie to a high shine, not considered practical like Jenny, but something mature, deep, and intensely interesting, like nature itself.

Thoughtful, at times she could stay utterly still and focused. He'd seen her sketch for hours while studying the most minute flower. Yet like a weathervane in a stiff breeze, she could change her manner and shriek over something exciting, running about, arms flapping. Then she would seem exactly like a young girl again.

It was vexing, and yet, he wouldn't change anything about her.

In fact, Eleanor seemed practically perfect. Gray had only to determine her feelings on certain matters, namely becoming attached to him and living in a small house on the Cambrey estate. She would be the wife of a seamstress's son, a man in service to the very same earl her older sister had married.

Or was she hoping for bigger, better things?

She was a baron's daughter, with sisters who hadn't simply married well. They'd both become countesses.

Would she be content? Or was she eager for next year's Season?
For all he knew, she might have a young man already sweet on her and with whom she, in turn, was enamored. She had said she'd found some interesting men in London.

Perhaps men who were titled or, at least, sons of the nobility.

Men her own age, no doubt. If he ruminated on it, she was probably a decade younger than his widow friend, although only eight years younger than himself, and a lifetime less cynical than his bluestocking bedmate.

Still, he had no business thinking of her in a romantic way.

The feelings warring within him were like nothing he'd ever experienced. Moreover, he had known this would happen if he ever gave in to the impulse to touch her.

Now, he had to decide if he were going to give in to his baser instincts when the next opportunity arose, or take the high road and treat her as the forbidden younger sister, as he would for any of his close friends. And Cam, Eleanor's brother-in-law, was the closest of all.

After a restless night, Gray was still pondering the issue of desiring Eleanor, while feeling he shouldn't want her at all, when he wandered into the morning room, following the aroma of bacon and sausages.

Eleanor wasn't there, but everyone else was except the two youngest who still ate in the nursery with the nanny.

"Good morning." Then before he could stop himself, he blurted, "Where is Miss Eleanor?"

"She ate already," Phoebe said, munching on toast. "She gets up very early for a girl."

He smiled. "So, she has gone for a walk?" Eleanor had a way of moving quietly, effortlessly across a meadow, her head up watching everything like an observant deer. It was a joy to watch, and he'd done so on many a sunny day at Turvey House while going about his duties.

"No," Lady Angsley said. "She didn't want to miss Beryl and Philip's departure. I believe she is with Beryl even now. You look thin, eat something," she ordered, changing the subject.

He smiled. Lady Angsley sounded like his mother when she said that, reminding him of his duty.

"I'll have something light and then go have tea with my mother. She knows I'm on the estate and wouldn't forgive me not stopping in first thing."

"You're a good son," Lady Angsley said. "Please take her whatever you think she might like from the buffet."

Thus, after toast and a coddled egg, he found himself heading to the granary lodge with a basket laden with food, both cooked items and some baked goods. He wasn't avoiding Eleanor, he told himself, as he hurried across the back lawn and then the pasture. He simply was delaying seeing her again, knowing how she affected him.

ELEANOR WATCHED THE CARRIAGE until it was out of sight. It carried away Beryl, Philip, and their curiously personable cat. Grayson had appeared a minute before their departure to hug Beryl and shake the captain's hand, and then he'd disappeared again while the rest of them said their goodbyes. Young Asher stared after the carriage, looking morose at the sea captain's departure.

Truthfully, she felt a little at loose ends, too, with Beryl gone.

Sighing, Eleanor wondered, *Now what?*

She hoped she would get a letter from Turvey House with some good news. Meanwhile, she'd put off her walk and now intended to take it. A watery sun was struggling to warm the earth a little, although clouds still hung over the landscape. She thought they looked beautiful.

With a cloak, her favorite straw hat, and her Wellingtons on again, she headed out the back, having got nearly as far as the first copse of trees when a figure seemed to appear from nowhere.

She gasped at the gnarled man who'd stepped from behind a birch, practically into her path.

CHAPTER SIX

"Where are you going, missy?" the old man demanded.

Momentarily surprised, Eleanor gaped before responding. "Simply a walk, sir."

Why she answered the brusque stranger, she had no idea.

"Be careful," he warned her.

"Of what?"

He cocked his head of white hair, his ruddy, lined farmer's face taking measure of her.

"Vicious foxes, for one. Though some say there are packs of wild dogs."

She hadn't heard of either, and, surely, someone from the hall would have told her if she needed to beware.

"I thank you for the warning. Good day."

She had to go around him since the old man hadn't yet moved. After she'd taken a few steps, he called out to her, "Missy!"

Hesitating, she waited.

"Don't go anywhere near the river, not if you know what's good for you."

"Why, sir?"

"It's a death-trap! All this rain has swollen her something fierce, and she's about to spill from her bed. When she crests, it'll be a sight to see, but only from afar. You'd be swept away and lost forever."

She shivered. He certainly had a way about him, but he obviously meant well.

"Thank you," she called out over her shoulder.

When he didn't respond, Eleanor turned around and nearly shrieked, for as he walked away, hanging down his back was a coarse burlap bag, stained red from the inside with what looked like blood.

Dear God, what was he carrying? And why was he going to Angsley Hall?

Wondering if she should go back, she tried to make sense of him and his sack when she recalled the happenings of the night before. The chickens, the dogs, and the farmer.

Realizing he was carrying evidence of Lord Angsley's spaniels' mischievous adventures, she shook her head at her own imagination.

She would try to remember to tell Lord and Lady Angsley at dinner how the Gothic tone of her visit had continued even this morning. Then she set out on a brisk walk, what her oldest sister Jenny called a prancing pace, all the while heeding the farmer's warning but wanting, at least, to see the River Great Ouse in all its majesty.

He'd been correct. The riverbed was full, and the water was moving more swiftly than she'd ever seen. As long as she stayed a few feet up the bank, however, she felt perfectly safe.

If the rain held off, she would bring her sketchpad the next time she walked, maybe even later in the day, and try to capture the beauty of raging nature. She wished she could sit for a while and watch, but the ground was wet. While her feet were kept dry by her boots, her cloak would do nothing to stop the rainwater from seeping from the ground through every layer.

Glancing around, Eleanor decided she could, perhaps, manage to climb onto a low branch and lean against the trunk. From such a perch, she was sure to see not only birds, but perhaps fish jumping, and other creatures coming to the water's edge.

To that end, she placed the toe of her boot in a crevice in the tree. Wishing her Wellie's were more pointed and not so uselessly round, she grabbed hold of the lowest branch in order to pull herself up.

A hand on her shoulder made her nearly shriek for the second time that morning. But Grayson's voice at the same time stopped the scream in her throat.

"What on earth are you doing?" he demanded.

GRAY HAD WATCHED HER as he'd approached. He'd left the house not long after she had, feeling a little anxious about her destination, particularly when Farmer McNeil arrived with the bloody evidence of the prior night's mischief of Lord Angsley's dogs. When the old man mentioned how the river was soon to crest, Gray hurried after her.

At first, Eleanor looked to be simply gazing around, quite responsibly and maturely, and then, to his surprise, she seemed to try to climb a wet, slick oak tree, whose branches all hung out over the raging Ouse.

He'd reached her as she was pulling herself up.

Without releasing her hold on the tree, she turned and looked over her shoulder, shooting him a grin that seemed to squeeze his heart.

"Perfect timing," she declared. "Can you give me a boost? Make your hands into a stirrup for me, will you? These boots aren't made for climbing so much as for mud puddles and stomping about."

Was she insane?

"Are you mad? No, I will not help you into a tree so you can fall to your death in the river. Release the branch at once."

Her mouth dropped open. "Are you serious?"

"Deadly." And he stepped forward, reaching up and disengaging her hands. "Look at your gloves, soaked and filthy." He still held her hands but turned them palm up for her inspection.

She did look down at them, then back at him. "You sound like a fussy old woman."

Ouch!

She yanked her hands free.

"Do you really think I would scoot out to the end of the branch *over* the river?"

"Well, I . . . I don't know what you might do."

She rolled her eyes. "I am not George or Iris," she protested, mentioning two of the youngest Angsleys. "I was simply going to sit right here in the crook of the branch, safely cradled as only a tree can do, and watch."

She crossed her arms over her chest, drawing his eyes there, despite everything interesting being hidden by her cloak.

"Quietly and alone," she added.

His gaze flew back up to hers.

"I see. My apologies, then. You're right. I should have known better. You've always handled nature very responsibly."

He looked around. "I bet the view is very good from up there, but I think we need to go up one more branch at least."

"We?" she repeated.

"Yes, I'll give you a hand up if you let me enter your tree paradise with you."

She smiled, and it was breathtaking. He knew at once he was going to fall hard in an irrevocable and forever way for Eleanor if he so much as even cracked open the door to his heart.

He had a notion it was already too late.

Then she did something entirely inappropriate yet perfectly sensible. She tossed open her cloak to reveal an ordinary day gown, and she reached between her legs to grab the hem at the back. This, she pulled up, and easily tucked into the waistband of her skirt, creating a pantaloon effect.

If her mother, Lady Blackwood, could see her, Gray knew she would be scandalized.

He grinned. "Good idea. That will make it much easier." On the other hand, he could see a portion of her stockinged legs, but only a few inches, because her boots came up nearly to her kneecaps.

"I should have worn my riding habit, although honestly, it doesn't make me feel any more able to muck about."

It would have been a good idea as the skirts were much fuller for draping over the pommel and the jumping head. As easily as riding in a saddle, she could have climbed the tree. Today, however, she would have to make do with his help.

Bending, he clasped his hands together and made a stirrup as she'd suggested. She hesitated only an instant before stepping onto his palms and attaining the first branch. His hands were now filthy and got more so as he scrabbled up beside her.

"You were right," she said. "We need to go one higher."

If they were going to do this harebrained plan, he would go up first and then help her to follow. Thus, by way of his climbing and then pulling her up as she needed, they went up two more branches.

"Oh, this is perfect," Eleanor exclaimed as she sat in front of him with a leg dangling down on either side of the branch and balanced between his legs so he could steady her.

Looking over her head to see the river, he agreed it was a magnificent view.

"It's just as if we're birds," she declared.

"As long as we don't attempt any flying," he said, then caught his breath as she wiggled in excitement, her rear end warming the front of him.

Naturally, he encircled her with his arms to keep her safe, and after a brief hesitation, she settled back against him as he leaned against the trunk.

Grayson would like to have said it was comfortable, but it wasn't. The front of him was on high alert and throbbing due to her glorious curves both in his arms and resting against him. The blood had left his head and gone to parts south, which he hoped to God she couldn't feel.

Moreover, at the back of him, a tree knot was pressed painfully into his spine, and the hard branch under him was numbing the flesh of his bottom and thighs.

Yet, he would have sat there forever if it pleased her. As it was, they stayed for about ten minutes in absolute silence, just watching. It was the most peaceful minutes he could ever remember, especially with a female.

"I'm ready for tea," she said suddenly and stretched.

If he hadn't been holding her, she might have toppled out of the tree for the uncaring way she stretched out her legs and arms. He had to grip the branch with his thighs to steady them both. *What a trusting nature she had!*

"Though I think I am more in the mood for coffee," she added.

Then Eleanor tried to twist in his arms to look at him. "I can't recall whether you like coffee."

"Stop moving," he ordered, nearly losing his balance. Then he looked down into her upturned face, realized his arms were around this fascinating, lovely woman whose round bottom was snugged against his crotch. *How wonderful was life!*

He could kiss her again. However, if they both closed their eyes, they might end up on the ground with broken limbs.

"Well?" she asked. "Do you?"

"What?" He couldn't remember her question as her brown eyes blinked up at him.

Had he ever seen more soulful eyes? And with such a flame of passion flickering in their depths, he could hardly breathe.

When he sunk into her the first time, exploring the peaks of desire with her, he wanted those eyes open and looking directly into his.

What a thought! His body and imagination were far ahead of his relationship with Eleanor Blackwood, already wanting to copulate with her, planning the moment he entered her. He needed the cold rainwater to wash over him and bring him back to reality.

"Coffee," she reminded him. "Do you like it?"

He frowned. She was so mesmerizing; he couldn't remember if he did or not.

"I think it's time to climb down. Parts of me are numb," he confessed. But definitely not all of him.

"Very well. I shall move forward so you can get your leg over, and then you can climb down, and I'll come after."

His plan exactly. If she slipped, he would steady her. If she fell, he would catch her and probably never let her go.

"Careful," he instructed, as she inched forward.

"Goodbye, tree," she said. Then more loudly, she called out, "Goodbye, birds. Until next time Mrs. Robin and Mr. Finch. Oh, Grayson, I saw a grouse yesterday."

She continued to talk as he got onto the next branch and held his arms up to assist. She didn't need his help, it was clear. Yet as she slid down onto the next branch, most of her body managed to touch most of his, and his hands ended up steadying her by clamping around her waist.

In fact, Eleanor climbed down expertly, following his lead. Soon, they were standing on the still damp, spongey ground. Close, too close.

"Come along," she said, stepping away from him, her dress still tucked up. "I'll race you."

Without further warning, she took off at a run toward the house.

Strange lady, he mused, chasing after her. They had a moment alone and could have easily snuck a kiss under the boughs of the oak, but she'd run off like a child.

Didn't she feel what he felt? Maybe she wasn't ready for a grown-up relationship, after all. Or maybe she'd decided a servant's son was not her destiny.

ELEANOR DASHED AWAY FROM the man who was making her heart pound and the rest of her body feel strangely as if it were on fire. Half a dozen times, she'd caught her breath while resting in his arms. And she was sure he could hear her heart thundering. She wanted to press farther back against him and rub her cheek on his clothing like a cat.

When they'd started climbing down, parts of him were touching parts of her. She had prattled on about whatever came into her head to keep from saying something stupid, like "kiss me, please" or "I believe I love you."

Then, she'd dropped to the ground nearly into his arms and had to run away before he saw her feelings plainly on her face. She'd never been good at prevaricating. In fact, she loathed those who could lie well. Her father had lied to her mother about something as mundane as their finances and, ultimately, left them all in grave peril. Lying, especially to someone you professed to care about, was evil.

"Wait, Eleanor," he called out behind her.

After a few exhilarating yards, she stopped and waited for him. Just hearing him freely use her given name was a thrill.

"Yes?" she asked him politely.

Would he say something endearing again, about how wonderful she was?

"Your dress. You ought to tidy yourself up and untuck it before we get closer. Anyone looking out the back windows might see you."

Glancing down, she realized she probably didn't look all that enticing. Most ladies didn't wear Wellies for a start, and there was bark stuck in her hosiery, and by the feel at the back of her, she'd torn them as well.

Tugging her hem out of her waistband, she let her skirts loose to fall in a hopelessly wrinkled mess around her legs.

"Oh, dear! Do you think anyone will notice?"

When he laughed, heat crept up her face.

"Turn around, all the way, let me take a look," he insisted.

She twirled in a slow circle so he could see all of her.

"The back of your gown is rather soggy and dirty, I'm afraid."

Feeling crestfallen, Eleanor considered her options. *If Lady Angsley saw her in such a state, might she think less of her? Doubtful.* Her ladyship was used to loud and messy children, except for Beryl, who was extremely ladylike.

More worrisome was the appearance she would make if she entered with Grayson with her skirt in a rumpled mess. The entire household might think the worst—that he'd compromised her, and she'd let him.

"Don't worry," he said, reading her thoughts upon her face. "We'll go visit my mother. She was a seamstress after all. Surely, she can make your dress look presentable."

"Whatever will *she* think?" Eleanor asked while already having changed direction toward the old granary lodge.

"She'll think you're an adventurous lass who does more than sit indoors and do needlepoint."

"True," she agreed. "I've never really been good at that, but I can sit for hours sketching or with a book."

"I know. I've seen you. You're a very good artist."

Her entire body suffused with warmth, and this time, not from embarrassment. Grayson thought her a good artist. *Very good.*

She decided she would reward him with a drawing of something he liked. *What did he like?*

"You're very fond of your horse, aren't you?"

"Yes. Why?" he asked as they strolled along.

"The one you rode here?"

"Actually, my favorite horse is back at Turvey House. I'd ridden him from London, so I left him to rest and rode another."

"Oh." That made things a little more difficult, although a horse was a horse except for its markings. As long as she knew if it was a male or a female.

"Tell me the name of your favorite horse. I'll tell you if I remember which one it is."

"Percy."

Hm. It had been nearly a year since she'd been to Maggie's country house and seen Grayson or his horse, but she recalled one he rode most often.

"Black gelding with a white blaze."

"That's him," he agreed.

Good. She could sketch from any of the horses in the Angsley stables, and then use her Staedtler oil pastel pencils to make it look like Percy.

However, before they reached Mrs. O'Connor's room, one of the servants from the hall intercepted them.

"Her ladyship has had us looking high and low for you, Mr. O'Connor. She's had word from the Earl of Cambrey."

"Apparently not high enough," Grayson muttered. He turned to Eleanor. "Would you like to continue to my mother's or...?" he trailed off, looking at her dress and shrugging slightly.

"No, never mind about my skirts. Let's go find out what John wrote."

CHAPTER SEVEN

"I hope I did not alarm you," Lady Angsley apologized, but when she saw the state of Eleanor, she looked quite alarmed herself.

Not knowing what else to do, Eleanor curtsied to her. "I was in a tree, my lady, watching the river. Grayson came and found me and brought me back safely."

Best to make it sound like an act of heroism. Then she realized with disgust how easily she'd fallen into prevaricating.

"Actually, that's not true precisely," she amended. "I wasn't *in* the tree when he found me, but since I was going up it anyway, he helped me climb and then helped me get back down."

Lady Angsley frowned, either not caring about the lengthy explanation or displeased with her guests.

"I see," she intoned. "I have no doubt one of our maids can clean and repair it, and there's always Grayson's mother."

"About the message from Turvey House," Grayson interjected, sounding impatient.

"Oh, yes! My husband's nephew says all is well with little Rose. Margaret doesn't seem feverish anymore, but she has been unable to keep down her food. Her stomach is in the midst of upheaval, and John says his is, too."

"And Cam's fever is also gone?" Grayson asked.

"Apparently so."

The three of them stood there a moment.

"Is that all?" Grayson persisted.

"Yes." Her ladyship gave a small shrug. "I told you I didn't mean to alarm you."

"Was there nothing specifically from my sister for me?" Eleanor hoped maybe Lady Angsley had simply neglected to mention it.

"No."

After another brief pause, her ladyship smiled invitingly. "Would you care to do some needlepoint with me? I believe Phoebe is also going to be in the drawing room working on a cushion."

Eleanor would rather go back to a stuffy London ballroom. At least there, she would be moving and drinking champagne or lemonade, but pricking one's fingers over and over to make an ugly cushion cover or wall hanging seemed ridiculous.

"Thank you, but I had best go change out of these clothes before I get any dirt on your furniture."

"That's fine. Phoebe and I shall still be at it for hours. You may join us after."

"Yes, of course." She could almost feel Grayson grinning at her attempts to get out of the needlepoint session. "You see, my lady, I was about to go into your extensive library and look for a book. I finished all those I brought during my long carriage ride."

"A book?" Her ladyship frowned, then she guessed, "Not one for needlepoint, Eleanor?"

"No, my lady."

"I'll meet you in the library," Grayson suggested. "I'm not one for needlepoint either."

Luckily, that made Lady Angsley smile.

"Very well. I will see you both at afternoon tea, unless you take lunch, in which case, I'll see you sooner."

And she sailed off in a billow of burgundy satin.

Grayson cocked his head. "You looked like you might gnaw your own hands off rather than use them for needle work."

"Was my dislike so evident?"

"I don't think she was offended. I'll see you in the library later."

Eleanor agreed. It seemed he was going to stick close, just as his mother and Beryl had hoped. Surely, he didn't think they could read a book together, though.

GRAY FOUND HIMSELF AWAITING Eleanor with eagerness. He was besotted. That much was plain. She was simply the best female company he had ever encountered, and he could see himself spending the rest of his days enjoying life with her.

He tried to read the book titles but couldn't focus until, after about ten minutes, she reappeared. She had not only changed into a clean, fawn-colored gown, she had tidied her hair. Gone was the loose bun from which most of her hair had escaped. Now, she wore it in a single thick plait.

"I had to take it down and comb some leaves and twigs out of it," she explained when she saw him looking at her braid. "And putting it back up seemed such a nuisance."

"You look lovely either way," he told her.

In truth, however, this style was more that of a young girl, and he was back to wondering about the difference in their ages.

Immediately, she went to the shelves and began perusing the leather spines.

"Don't you adore a library? It is the next best thing to being outdoors. And while I usually prefer the smells of grass and flowers to anything indoors, I admit, I love the aroma of books."

"The aroma of books?" *What an unusual thing to say.*

"Yes, open one and get a good whiff of it. Here, try it." She pulled one off the shelf, noted its title, opened it, and stuck it in his face so the page touched the end of his nose.

"Yes, I suppose." This particular book smelled like a mix between used hay from the stables and a musty basement, but he would agree to practically anything she said.

He watched her, fascinated, as she pressed it to her own nose and rather loudly breathed in its aroma. Then Eleanor sneezed daintily.

"You're eight years younger than I am, I believe," he said.

"I'm not certain since I don't know your age. But if that's true, then it is soon to be only seven." She crouched down to look at books on the lowest shelf. He bent, too, so he could keep talking to her easily.

"Why? Is your birthday coming up?"

"Yes, next week. I was supposed to be celebrating it, as much as anyone does at my age, with my sister this year. No matter. If I'm still here, we can talk the Angsleys' cook into making a cake as easily as the Cambreys' cook."

"True." Still, it was probably a disappointment to her not to be with Maggie, Cam, and little Rosie. She could go home to be with her mother, older sister, and her husband, but she was undoubtedly holding out hope she could soon go to Turvey House.

He could try to make her birthday a special day in any case.

Next, she read off the names of a few books he'd heard of, *Gulliver's Travels*, *Tom Jones*, *Clarissa*, some of Dickens' works, and a Shakespeare collection in one volume. The Angsleys had a good library although he had only gone in once or twice, looking for a book on horse-breeding or some equally practical matter.

"Oh," she exclaimed.

"What have you found?"

"*Northanger Abbey.*"

"Another of your Gothic novels?" He liked her choice in the unusual and the dark macabre, rather than an insipid novel of manners. When he did read for entertainment, he tended toward travel stories but had run into a few Gothic tales.

She pulled the book out and ran a hand over its cover before opening it and flipping its pages.

"Not strictly. It has all the elements, but Miss Austen was writing a parody. Still, it's a very interesting story."

"Then you've already read it."

"Only once, and it was so enjoyable, I look forward to reading it again." She placed it on the round, polished library table before going back to the shelves.

"Here's one I've never read at all. *The Necromancer* by Flammenberg. He's German, and it's supposed to be very scary."

He watched her do an exaggerated little shiver.

"And this one," she said. "Mrs. Radcliffe's *A Sicilian Romance*. In an essay, she said she tried to evoke terror, not horror, which she looked down upon as causing one to freeze, thereby stunting the reader's faculties. On the other hand, terror, she said, stimulated the reader with imagination. I agree with her, and she so superbly causes one to feel terror in her stories. Do you agree with the distinction?"

"Yes, I think I do," Grayson said, reminded of a literature class from boarding school. "However, I am not sure, Professor Blackwood, if I could make the distinction myself."

She offered him her lovely smile.

All at once, he thought of a gift—perhaps the perfect birthday gift for her.

"The other evening you said you hadn't yet read Edgar Allan Poe, is that right?"

"I haven't yet come across one of his tales in any bookshop. Just bad luck, I suppose. I take it you've read him."

"I have read some of his stories and even some of his poetry. I believe you would enjoy him, though he tends a little more toward the horror."

"That's no matter. I would welcome the chance to read someone new to me. He only died a few years ago, I believe."

"Yes, would you go light the extra lamp, and then we'll see if we can find anything by him."

"But it's broad daylight," she pointed out.

"Then maybe you could open the other curtains. You know I am old enough to be your father, and my eyes aren't what they used to be."

She laughed. "I'm sorry I said that. You know I didn't mean it." But she got up and did what he asked.

When her back was turned, Grayson slipped a slim volume off the shelf and tucked it into his pocket, confident it was the only copy in the library.

"Is that better?" she asked.

"Yes, what little sunlight we have can now stream in. Come, help me look for something by Poe."

After a few minutes, when their search turned up nothing, he said, "I give up. How about we go riding before lunch and then dine with my mother? She will be thrilled."

"All right," Eleanor agreed, rising from where she'd ended up on the floor and then stretching.

He could not take his gaze from her as her lithe form bent this way and that, her lush curves visible through the cotton of her gown. Suddenly, his mouth had grown dry.

"If we are riding, I guess I had better change again," she said. "I'll take these books upstairs, too. If you pick out a good horse for me, I'll meet you down at the stables."

"With your antics around here," Grayson told her, "I think you should wear your riding habit at all times."

She made a face at him as he gestured for her to precede him out of the room. At the same time, he fingered the book in his pocket, a Poe collection of stories including *The Gold Bug*. Quietly pleased with himself, Gray followed after her.

ELEANOR DIDN'T LIKE TO benefit from her sister's illness. Yet now she had accepted the idea of not going directly to Turvey House, she was enjoying herself. If she was truly honest, she would have to say she liked being in the company of Grayson and having him mostly to herself for the first time in the years she'd known him.

She had made one massive error, and he had forgiven her. The day before, after an exhilarating ride, when at lunch with his mother, Eleanor had brought up Grayson's father, asking about the deceased Mr. O'Connor.

After all, why did something ordinary like a man living and then dying have to be shrouded in mystery? she wondered.

However, when Grayson's mother became visibly flustered, looking neither at her son nor at Eleanor, but keeping her head down absently stirring her tea, she knew she'd made a terrible error.

At once, Eleanor had apologized to both of them.

"It's all in the past," Mrs. O'Connor said quietly, while Grayson said naught at all. Thus, Eleanor had learned nothing new and had caused discomfort to her lunch hosts.

Afterward, as she and Grayson walked back to Angsley Hall, she again apologized.

"It's not your fault," he said. "Anyone would be curious. I am, but she has never said a word about him and told me she never will."

"And Lord and Lady Angsley know nothing about your father?"

Just then, four spaniels came running over the lawn.

"I need to speak to his lordship about their stable boy," Grayson said, sounding annoyed. "Either he's in charge of these dogs or he's not."

She assumed then, he would change the subject, but he added, "I have asked Lord Angsley about my sire, and he said my mother was about to give birth when she came here, directed to come to the estate by my father. Somehow, he knew the family would take her in and give her work. She said he was already dead when she arrived."

Eleanor gasped. "I'm sorry. I had no idea. Not only did I think your father was a servant here, I thought your father died when you were young. I didn't realize he passed before you were even born."

Grayson shrugged. "I've been surrounded by love and acceptance all my life. And importantly, by great men who helped guide me, including both of the Angsley brothers, Beryl's father, Harold, and Cam's father, Gideon, before the earl passed. I don't believe I have lacked for anything."

She nodded. "I am glad. Your father was a good man to direct your mother here. This family is generous and welcoming. I've certainly experienced that."

He fell silent for a moment.

"Would you like to help me repay them in a small way?"

"Yes," she said. "What do you intend?"

"Lord Angsley is secretly a bit of an amateur entomologist."

"He likes bugs? I've never heard him mention it."

"As I said, it's a secret because Lady Angsley would not approve or appreciate it. In any case, there's a beetle, native to England, said to be a beautiful golden color."

"Gold?"

"Yes. You know how dragonflies are iridescent. Well, this beetle has a coating of such strange golden shine, it looks like actual gold. If we could find one, he would be most appreciative."

Eleanor considered it. Hunting a gold bug would be like seeking treasure.

"I've seen shiny green beetles before. They do have a golden tinge sometimes. Would that do?" If Lord Angsley would be happy with such, she would be thrilled to provide it.

He nodded, looking thoughtful. "Perhaps it would. Maybe we can find one less green and more gold."

"It would give us something productive to do, and we could be outdoors, which you know I enjoy. Moreover, I could bring my sketchbook."

"But not a word to anyone," Grayson insisted.

"All right. We shall keep our quest between the two of us," she agreed, enjoying the idea of a shared secret. "How shall we begin?"

"Tomorrow morning, first thing. I'll meet you in the library after breakfast. By then, I will have taken the liberty of drawing a picture—"

"I didn't know you could sketch," she interrupted him.

"Nothing like you, but I can probably draw a beetle so it doesn't look like a cat."

They laughed.

"This will be great fun," she said.

He shot her an indecipherable look, making her insides tremble. *Was he up to mischief?*

"I'm sorry I raised my voice to you the other day," Grayson confessed all of a sudden. "I don't think you're a selfish person at all."

Eleanor shook her head. *How could he still be thinking of such an insignificant incident?*

"It was already forgotten and forgiven," she said, feeling her cheeks warm.

"I was simply worried you would go to Turvey House against everyone's wishes and fall ill." After a brief pause, he added, "I couldn't bear that."

What could she say to that?

"Thank you." She was more determined than ever to create a beautiful sketch for him. "Speaking of sketching, I'm going to do a little drawing while the light is good."

"You won't climb anything, will you?" he asked, and she feared he was going to stick close to her as if she were a toddlekins in leading strings.

"No, I'll keep my feet on the ground."

Or no higher than a fence railing, she thought, *or maybe the ladder in the stables.*

"Very well," he agreed. "I have a few things to do, as well."

He paused, and she had the insane notion he wished to kiss her farewell. They stared at each other, and she would have leaned toward him and let him, if they'd been in a secluded spot.

Then the moment filled with stirring anticipation passed, and they went their separate ways for the remainder of the afternoon.

CHAPTER EIGHT

Getting Eleanor to come to the library had been relatively easy. Now, Gray hoped he could pull off the trickery he'd learned from Poe. He'd easily procured a piece of vellum from Lord Angsley's writing desk, and the night before, he had drawn everything he needed on one side. Yet, to the eye, it appeared blank.

He rubbed his hands together with glee, feeling like an excited child pulling off a particularly good prank. He was no scientist and hadn't much of a clue what Poe was writing about in the lines from *The Gold Bug*, "Zaire, digested in aqua regia, and diluted with four times its weight of water," or "the regulus of cobalt, dissolved in spirit of nitre."

Grayson only knew he needed to create invisible ink, which he did quite well with lemon juice as he had with Cam when they were boys, writing secret messages to each other for fun.

And now, he waited.

Eleanor entered looking lovely. Her own beauty was even more apparent for the lack of adornment or accessories on her plain gown of forest green.

Still, he couldn't help thinking she would look better in nothing at all.

"I said good day," came her voice, and he realized she must have spoken already, and like a buffoon, he had missed her greeting. His tongue was probably hanging out, as well.

"Sorry, I was thinking of the day ahead."

"I'm eager to see your drawing of the gold bug." She drew close and sat down opposite him.

"I decided to wait for you to help me draw it. And I found this natural history book on the shelf."

He had it open to a page with beetles.

"This one is close enough, I think." He lay his finger on the beetle that looked like a scarab.

"It's not gold," she pointed out. "Nor do I have a colored pencil that could realistically make it appear so."

"That's fine. We'll just sketch out a beetle and take it with us."

"But I know what a beetle looks like," she protested.

"They come in all shapes and sizes." He pushed the book toward her. At the same time, he slid his paper out from under it. "We're not looking for a wasp beetle or a ladybird. Only this type, perhaps. See, the flower chafer comes in gold, but only very rarely."

Then he flipped the paper over so she could see there was no writing on either side, flipping it again, tapping his pencil from his pocket on the paper, drawing her attention to the blankness of its entirety.

Then, he began to draw, making sure he was on the truly clean side of the paper, drawing in the spot he'd already determined mimicked the image he'd drawn on the other side. In a few moments, he'd sketched a crude beetle with little antennae and an exaggerated shape to its body.

"The beetle we're looking for looks like—"

"A skull," she interrupted.

Goodness, she caught on quickly.

"Yes," he said, as if only just noticing. "I suppose, except for the appendages, it does."

"Maybe *I* should have drawn it." Then Eleanor chuckled. "I mean no disrespect to your sketching abilities."

"None taken."

Now came the tricky part. Just then, as planned, one of the maids brought in a tray of piping hot coffee, with the pot set on a metal trivet.

"I recalled you like coffee sometimes." And without waiting for a reply, he lifted the pot, poured them each a cup, and instead of replacing the pot on the trivet, he set it elsewhere on the silver tray. Then he picked up the paper, pretending to study it, and in a moment, set it down on the iron trivet.

Hopefully, it would be hot enough to activate the lemon juice with which he'd written his secret message on the back side of the seemingly blank paper.

"Let's see if there is another book on the shelf with bugs. I didn't look all that thoroughly. Perhaps if we know the habitat, it will be easier to find. For instance, does it live on flowers or deep in the forest on rotten wood? Or do we need to dig in the dirt or perhaps go to a cave?"

"Indeed," she said. "That would be good to know."

For a few minutes, they looked for natural history books, found one or two, discounted their usefulness, and then finally gave up.

"We should drink the coffee before it grows cold," he said, waiting for her to pick up her cup.

Leaning over the table, she gasped, and Grayson felt a surge of triumph as she reached out slowly and took hold of the paper. He could even see it was shaking slightly in her grasp, which meant her hand was trembling.

"What on earth?" she asked.

"What?" He had taken hold of his coffee cup and feigned ignorance.

"Do you not see what I see?" she demanded.

"Are you going to make fun of my beetle drawing again?"

"No, Grayson, look." And Eleanor stuck the vellum under his nose.

"By God, you were right, my beetle does look exactly like a skull, more so than I could have imagined."

"I don't think that is your beetle," she said, her voice breathy with wonder. "And look, there are other markings on the paper."

"Good God!" he exclaimed. "What is all that?"

Setting down his cup, he snatched the paper from her and examined it.

Instead of merely his ugly beetle, which was visible on the other side, there was now a drawing of a skull, a "death head" as Poe had described it in his tale, sketched in a murky brown ink.

"And what is that?" He pointed diagonally to the other edge in case she hadn't noticed it.

"It looks like a goat," she said.

"But so small," he pointed out. "Like a baby goat, or a kid, don't you think?" He had certainly tried to evoke a kid, at any rate. "And then, what is all that gibberish in between?"

She took it back from him, then she walked to the window. Today was another overcast day, yet still, there was a bright steely light.

"You're right. There are lines of nonsense text between the goat—"

"Kid," he interrupted.

"And the skull," she said. "I can make neither heads nor tails of it."

He walked to her side and studied it with her, able to sniff the delightful floral scent of her *eau de toilette*.

He thought he'd done a rather good job. For clearly, although faint, he could see four lines of numbers and symbols, starting with "53 + + ! 3 0 5)) 6 * ; 4 8 2 6) 4 + .) 4 +) ; 8."

"Whatever can it mean?" she mused. "It must be a puzzle, don't you think?"

She looked up at him, and they were so close, he could see the reflection of the clouds in her brown eyes.

He nodded. He would have agreed with whatever words came out of her luscious mouth at that moment.

She flipped the paper over, and there was his beetle.

"How strange! It looks so much like the skull, as if you invoked the image on the other side by drawing your ugly bug."

He couldn't help smiling at her assessment of his beetle.

"How can one invoke something onto paper?" he teased. "By magic?"

"It would seem so. I saw the paper a few minutes ago, and it was blank except for your drawing. Where did this come from? It's giving me goosebumps."

He glanced at her arm. It looked perfectly smooth to him.

"Where did you get this sheet of paper?" she asked.

"That is a good question. I didn't have a sketchpad at my disposal as you do, so I hunted around in here. I was about to ask Lord Angsley when I saw a book sticking out a little farther than the others on the shelf. I was only going to push it back in, but instead, I pulled it out because of the title."

He went to the shelf and from amongst a number of large, thick volumes whose spines were nearly identical, he drew the one he'd found the night before and held it before her.

"I imagine, as an ambassador for her queen, Lord Angsley had an interest in the subject," he told her.

She glanced down at the massive book in his hands with a reddish-brown spine and a deep-green leather cover, and read the title, "*A Complete Collection of State Trials and Proceedings for High Treason and Other Crimes and Misdemeanors.*"

"Volume fourteen," he added, because he'd memorized it.

She laughed. "Unquestionably, one of the longest titles I've ever seen." Glancing up at him, she asked, "And it grabbed your interest enough to pull the book from the shelf among all the other volumes with the *exact* same title?"

Was she doubting his ridiculous story?

He shrugged. "It seemed to be calling to me by the fact of it being stuck out a little. It caught my shoulder as I went by." In truth, he'd searched for an hour looking for a book that mentioned the pirate Captain Kidd, and this boring looking volume was the only one. In fact, stumbling upon Kidd in volume fourteen had been a godsend.

She frowned, then looked down at the book again. "I've been in a bookshop and felt as if a book were 'calling' to me, as you put it."

Inside, he sighed with relief. The jig was not up yet!

"The blank paper was stuck in the book," he told her. "Would you like to see where?"

She nodded, so he placed it upon the table. While she watched him flip it open to the table of contents, she laughed again.

"It has over thirteen hundred pages!"

"No, not really," he told her. "Only half that. Each page has two columns and thus, two numbers. It is easier for the eye to read quickly down a column than to go all the way across a full page, especially of a book this tall and wide. I think that's why it was printed in such a manner."

"That makes good sense," she agreed.

"The paper that has mysteriously shown a deathly skull image was here." He ran his finger down the contents list and read aloud, "The Trial of Captain William Kidd, at the Old Bailey, for Murder and Piracy upon the High Seas."

"Gracious! A pirate," Eleanor said enthusiastically. "If only Philip were here to comment on our strange findings."

Gray was glad Philip wasn't there, for that would mean Beryl would be there, too. And as much as he adored the woman who was like a sister to him, if she'd been there, then he would definitely not have Eleanor all to himself.

"The paper was right there, sticking out a little higher than the book's pages between columns 123/124 and

125/126. It was blank, or seemingly so, and I took it thinking no one would mind."

"I suppose, since the book belongs to his lordship, we should ask him about it. Maybe he can—"

"That would only lead to questions, and before you know it, we would have to tell him about our quest," Gray reminded her.

"I'm not entirely sure the initial quest is important anymore. Do you realize what this is?"

Gray had to hide the smile that threatened to overtake his expression. Trying to look unwitting, he widened his eyes.

"No, what?"

"I think it is a puzzle about Captain Kidd, and any puzzle about a pirate must lead to his treasure. I've read *Robinson Crusoe*!" she proclaimed.

Picking up the piece of paper, she studied it. "You must be correct. It is a baby goat, a kid, and the skull in the other corner is a seal, a pirate's stamp, if you will."

"You know, you might be right," he said. "But what on earth are we to make of the nonsense lines?"

"I think they are in code." Her voice took on a note of excitement. "Obviously, since Kidd was an Englishman—"

"Actually, he was Scottish."

She blinked at him, and he wished he'd kept his mouth shut. His knowing too much about the pirate would assuredly tip her off that this wasn't random and coincidental.

"Is that common knowledge?" she asked. Then she shook her head. "Never mind, the pun of the baby goat is in English, so we'll assume the puzzle is in English, too."

"Good idea," he agreed, vowing to let her lead from now on and not ruin the game.

Suddenly, she squealed.

"What is it?" he asked, slightly alarmed. She sounded exactly like a youngster.

"It's very exciting, that's all." And, to his surprise, she stretched up on her toes and kissed his cheek.

Nice, but not exactly satisfying.

Without thinking of anything except her nearness and her gorgeous eyes and lips, and her delightful scent, Gray drew her close and claimed her mouth under his.

If she wanted "very exciting," then a peck on the cheek was not the right type of kiss.

Slanting his mouth, he tested her readiness for more by touching his tongue to her upper lip. He felt her body tense a moment before she relaxed against him and parted her lips.

Gently, he slid his tongue inside her sweet mouth, and she gasped slightly, which only drew him in farther. Then, ever so slightly, she touched his tongue with her own.

"Mmm," he murmured.

Next thing he knew, she'd reached her hands around the back of his neck and was holding him to her, with her fingers in his hair.

He grasped her waist, pulling her up against his body and, with their tongues dancing in earnest, he kissed her until every nerve in his body seemed to be burning.

Was it possible blood could run hot? He didn't know, but it felt as though he was on fire for Eleanor Blackwood, and the only thing that could put it out was taking off all her clothes—and, of course, his own—and seeking relief by becoming one with her.

At the notion of her naked beneath him, her silky hair spread about her lovely face, her shoulders and breasts laid bare for him to nibble and suck, he could hardly breathe or hear anything but his own pounding heart.

His hands drifted from her waist to her bottom, squeezing gently, making her gasp again, even as he drew her up against his throbbing body.

Christ, but he was ready for her! His mind and soul were filled with Eleanor and, in turn, he wanted to fill her.

"Gray," she said, pulling back slightly.

"Eleanor," he returned, biting his tongue to keep from apologizing because he knew it irked her when he did so.

Besides, he didn't feel sorry. Not even a little. He wanted to do it again. What's more, he fully intended to do so when the library door swung open.

CHAPTER NINE

Shocked, Eleanor and Grayson both stood, frozen, their heads turned in unison, his hands on her behind, hers around his neck.

Luckily, it was only Phoebe, whose eyes grew as big as dinner plates.

"I . . . I . . . I," she tried three times.

By then, he and Eleanor had parted.

Before either of them could say anything, Phoebe backed out the door and closed it firmly.

"Oh, dear!" Eleanor said. "What do you think we should do?"

"I suppose one of us should go find her and talk to her," he suggested.

"One of us?" she asked, tilting her head, offering him a wry smile.

"Probably you since I might be seen as threatening."

She blinked at him. "I don't feel threatened."

He liked the new, husky tone to her voice as she flirted with him.

"That's because I want to kiss you, not order you to keep quiet."

"True," she agreed. "And it would be better coming from me. I may have to bribe her, too. Beryl once gave Phoebe a boiled sweet to keep her from telling Lord and Lady Angsley how we'd made Asher sneak into the cellar and steal a bottle of wine for us."

"What happened?"

"Poor Asher, he succeeded, and so we had to let him drink with us. He got very sick. Phoebe found us and threatened to tell."

Grayson couldn't help laughing. "Did she hold her tongue when bribed?"

"She did, as far as I know. I had best go find her now."

He nodded.

"Don't work on the puzzle without me," Eleanor begged.

"I wouldn't dream of it. I promise."

She rushed to the door. When she reached it, with her hand on the latch, she turned.

"I very much enjoyed the kiss, by the way, and would like to do it again."

Then she left.

Was he playing with her emotions? Toying with her heart?

He thought about it long and hard. No, he was perfectly serious about Eleanor Blackwood. In that moment, he decided what the treasure at the end of the game would be.

THERE HAD BEEN NO opportunity to meet with Grayson in the library before dinner. First, Eleanor spent ages with Phoebe, agreeing to answer questions truthfully in exchange for the girl's silence. It seemed an easy bargain until she discovered Phoebe had many questions—about boys, babies, London, dancing, the Season, and more.

She expressly wanted to know about kissing, and Eleanor found herself giving a first-hand account, toned down for the girl's younger ears, of what it was like. She would have liked to be alone, perhaps lying peacefully in a meadow, recalling how it felt to have Grayson not only kiss her but touch her tongue with his. Even thinking of it made her stomach twitch.

And when his hands grasped her bottom, he certainly shocked her at first. Then his squeezing fingers had made her tingle all over. For a brief moment, she remembered how he'd pulled her against his male parts, which were hard. Rather than being scary, she had wanted more.

Of course, she didn't tell Phoebe any of that. Perhaps, in a few years, she would give the girl a copy of a helpful book. She and Beryl had read more than one which had opened their eyes to what happened between men and women.

Eventually, Eleanor fled the girl's room, promising to have another heart-to-heart talk in a few days. Then she had run directly into Lady Angsley who sighed about missing her eldest child before saying how glad she was to have Eleanor there, "almost like having Beryl."

With those kind words, she could hardly turn her ladyship down when asked to go for a long stroll. Eleanor used the time to ask about any beetles Lady Angsley might have seen since the woman was a devoted gardener. That led her hostess to give an extended discourse on every flower in her terraced beds.

When even Eleanor was tired of hearing about the natural world, she excused herself. She wanted to get her sketch pad and begin her drawing of Grayson's horse.

By the time she had a rather good illustration of a horse sketched and shaded, she looked up from her perch on a bale of hay in the stables to see Mrs. O'Connor happening by.

"Good day," she called out to Grayson's mother.

Turning and waving, Mrs. O'Connor changed direction from walking toward the main house to the open paddock gate.

"Good day, Miss Eleanor. And it is a lovely one after so much rain. What have you got there?"

Suddenly, Eleanor felt a little shy. What would Mrs. O'Connor think about her creating a drawing for Grayson? She turned the pad so his mother could see.

The woman studied it a moment, then she looked over at the horse, then she looked at Eleanor.

"I'm sorry. I can see *that* horse plain as day," Mrs. O'Connor gestured to the one beyond the fence, "but this one is a bit blurry without my spectacles. Still, they don't look the same at all. With the blaze on its nose, your drawing looks more like Gray's Percy."

"You're correct. He told me Percy was his favorite."

His mother looked again, then she smiled. "He'll love it. It's very sweet of you to make this for him."

Eleanor felt the heat rise to her cheeks. If only she were better at hiding her emotions.

"He has been ever so kind to stay and keep me company after Beryl left." She had to glance away from his mother's gaze when her mind started to consider their kissing, but her skin grew warm, nonetheless.

"I won't interrupt you any longer," Mrs. O'Connor said. "I'm on my way to the main house to have tea with Cook while the younger ones prep the fixings for tonight's meal. I wish I could invite you along, but the kitchen staff would go barmy if you were to sit at their table. They wouldn't know what to do with themselves."

"I understand," Eleanor said. "I shall have to go in soon and dress for dinner anyway. Enjoy your tea."

Mrs. O'Connor strode off, a very fit woman in her late forties, perhaps early fifties, who, if not for her failing eyesight, could have served at the main house for decades to come. How fortunate her son lived so close.

Thinking of Grayson, Eleanor sketched in the detail of the back hooves and then closed her pad and headed in the same direction as his mother had taken. While many hours stretched ahead of her before bedtime, it would be difficult to spend time alone with him after dinner in the library, for guests were expected to be social and to participate in games or provide entertainment if one could sing or play an instrument.

Eleanor couldn't beg off for the sake of sitting in a corner trying to decipher a cryptic message from a dead pirate. Her rudeness would be inexcusable.

The rain, which had held off all day, started just as they sat down to dinner and continued. It was coming down in sheets by the time the merry party gathered in the drawing room for cards and charades.

Eleanor managed to stump them with riddles about time, a windmill, and even a teapot, all memorized from her tattered copy of *Food for the Mind* by the secretive John the Giant Killer, Esq. She long-suspected "John" was really a quick-witted woman but couldn't prove it.

When Grayson guessed her last riddle about the sun, they were all beginning to yawn, and it was time to retire. As she left the room, he caught up with her at the foot of the stairs. It was the first time they'd spoken privately since the kiss.

"Shall we get back to Captain Kidd's mystery first thing in the morning?" he asked.

"I can hardly wait." She wondered if they would also kiss again, but that was hardly something she could simply ask. "Where is the paper?"

"I put it back in the book for safekeeping, as it seems no one has looked at those volumes for years."

"Very well. I'll see you in the morning."

But she couldn't simply turn and go upstairs, knowing he was following her with his eyes. Nor could they go up together.

When she hesitated, they locked gazes, and she could see numerous thoughts flickering behind his dark eyes. If she knew precisely what passion looked like, she would swear she saw it, along with merriment and myriad other emotions.

A slight softening of his lips, a crinkling of the corners of his eyes, and in his expression, a hidden message meant only for her.

"Good night," he said, turning away and disappearing down the passageway to the back of the house. Lord Angsley was still milling about somewhere. Maybe the two men would smoke cigars and drink brandy.

Eleanor wanted to follow him, but she did the responsible thing and went to bed. Unfortunately, hours later, she still lay awake, listening to the rain. She'd been unable to relax her mind, thinking of how amazing the appearance of the markings on the paper and how even more amazing was Grayson's kiss.

Getting out of bed, she opened her drapes a little to enjoy the lightning show, feeling the hair on the back of her neck stand up when thunder boomed, seemingly directly over Angsley Hall. A moment later, a brilliant, blinding flash split the blackness. She was momentarily blinded.

Strangely, she imagined she heard the whinny of a horse, but no rider would be out in this weather. It was worse than the night Grayson arrived.

Was it possible the sound had carried from the stables?

Sighing, she considered continuing to read one of the books from the library. Picking up *The Necromancer*, she opened it to where she'd left off. Then she tossed it onto the bed. Instead of reading about the strange and unusual, Eleanor decided she would rather indulge herself in a real-life mystery.

Wrapping herself in her dressing gown and reaching for her lamp, she tiptoed along the hallway and went quietly downstairs. The house seemed larger and the ceiling higher in the pitch black of night. A delicious shiver raced up her spine, and for a moment, she could imagine she was wandering the halls of the castle of Otranto or of Udolpho. All she needed was a good strong draft to blow out her lamp, and the setting would be complete.

Soon, however, she was in the tidy, modern library setting her lamp on the table to chase the gloomy shadows. She lit two other lamps, and then found volume fourteen, relieved to see the paper safely tucked between the pages about Captain Kidd's trial.

Eleanor couldn't wait to dive back into the puzzle and discover if the gibberish really were instructions leading to his treasure. Surely, a simple map would have been easier, but then, she supposed, anyone could find the buried gold and jewels.

Perhaps Lord Angsley bought the book from a London merchant who got the book from someone who placed that mysterious paper in it after attending the pirate's trial or his execution. Maybe this same someone got the paper directly from William Kidd or created the puzzle as instructed without even knowing what it really said.

Hopefully, Grayson wouldn't be angry with her for forging ahead on her own, but instead, pleased with any discoveries she made. To that end, she studied the seemingly random letters. If they did make up words, which she was positive they did, then some of them would repeat, the vowels, for instance, more than any other.

Did she know this to be true?

Off the closest shelf, she grabbed the first book she put her fingers on, which turned out to be James Boswell's acclaimed *The Life of Samuel Johnson*. Eleanor studied a paragraph, then another, and then another. She was right. The letter *e* showed up more than any other letter.

Perhaps if she figured out which of the numbers or symbols was most used in the brief passage, she could mark them as an *e* for the time being. She should have brought some blank paper, not wishing to mark upon the original.

Luckily, she was in the library with a writing desk. To her delight, it was stocked full of paper, pens, and pencils.

Why had Grayson not been able to find paper when he was looking for a sheet the other day? If he had found some, he might never have looked in Volume XIV and discovered Kidd's puzzle. *How fortuitous!*

She set to work making a list of the characters, finding there were thirty-three instances of the number eight.

"I shall make each of them an *e*," she said aloud. It made perfect sense, especially when she saw five double eights, which she decided must stand for *ee*, perhaps indicating such words as *seen* or *meet*.

The next most prevalent character in the puzzle was a semi-colon, yet it didn't seem to be used as punctuation. It was undoubtedly code for another letter; however, she couldn't decide what letter appeared the most after an *e* in the English language. Perhaps an *a*.

"Maybe a *t* or an *o*," she muttered.

If she got off on the wrong track now, it could be disastrous. Spending a few more minutes creating a list of all the characters in order of how many were in the puzzle, she then copied out the puzzle again on her paper, writing the letter *e* above each of the eights. It was a start.

Yawning, Eleanor realized she ought to get some sleep if she were to rise early enough to meet Grayson in the library before breakfast, and undeniably, some rest would sharpen her mind to help solve the puzzle.

After putting everything back as she'd found it and slipping her new sheet of paper into the pocket of her wrap, Eleanor turned down the two lamps, and then picked up her own.

Outside the library, all was quiet until—*bang*! She jumped, startled, and then froze at the loud sound that had come from the other end of the hallway, somewhere toward the back of the house. Her heart quickened.

She waited a moment, and all was silent. Just as she breathed a sigh—*bang!*—she heard it again.

"Oh, dear," she said, despite realizing it wasn't a gunshot this time. Something more benign, like a…

Her brain couldn't fill in anything. She could go upstairs and ignore the dreadful noise, or she could investigate.

Choosing the latter, as she trod along the passageway toward the rear of the house, one thing became uncomfortably clear—the floor was wet. She held her lamp down low to see it was merely water, although a little muddy, as if someone had come in from the outside.

She was certain it hadn't been there at bedtime. Someone had been out in the storm. *How strange!*

Bang! Taking a deep, fortifying breath, thinking she could hear her own heartbeat, Eleanor continued along the wet hallway, getting her kidskin slippers damp.

Bang! Eleanor approached the window overlooking the garden. The shutter had blown loose and was now making a merry racket as it slammed shut before swinging open again.

She laughed with relief and set her lamp down on the wooden floor beside her before working to open the window sash, which, if properly maintained, should easily slide upward. It did. Eight glass panes over eight moved fluidly under her touch, and she reached out, even as a gust of wind blew rainwater all over her and snuffed out her oil lamp.

"Drat!" she exclaimed. It was damnably cold water, too.

In a moment, she had managed to secure the shutter with its clever little hook. As she closed the window, however, Eleanor felt rather than saw the presence of someone nearby. The hair on her neck arose, as did gooseflesh upon her arms.

The scuffling of a shoe upon the floor alerted her to the unknown person's proximity, and suddenly, arms went around her.

"I've got you," an unfamiliar voice exclaimed.

CHAPTER TEN

Eleanor struggled, feeling the tall stranger's bony arms tighten.

"Let me go," she yelled, lashing out, even as terror filled her, making her want to run and scream.

Surprisingly, the arms dropped away from her instantly.

"Miss Eleanor?" came a bewildered voice, and then she recognized it.

"Mr. Stanley?" *The butler, of course!*

"Why are you creeping in the window?" the Angsley butler asked, sounding flabbergasted. Then, as if recalling his place, he added, "Not that it is any of my business, miss."

Everything would make sense with some light, she assumed.

"Somewhere on the floor is my lamp," she told him, and they immediately bumped heads as they both bent down to find it.

"Ow," she said.

"My apologies, miss." In another moment, he said, "I have found it."

When he relit it, she nearly yelled again. For in the scant light flickering from below, the butler's face looked skeletal, and his eye sockets appeared very large and dark, almost as if sunken.

She shuddered, probably from the cold rain that had spattered her face and neck. Moreover, he was not dressed for going to bed, but rather, wearing an oil skin and Wellingtons. Even stranger, they were perfectly dry, so he could not have caused the water in the front hallway.

How many people were up and wandering in and out of Angsley Hall?

As he dropped a handy box of matches back into his pocket, she thought she'd better explain herself, despite dying to ask him where he was going on such a night and at such a late hour.

"I was awake," she told him, "and I heard the shutter slamming against the house."

He nodded. "Thank you, miss. I was just coming to do the same." Then he looked down at the puddle. "I'll get the maid to clean that up before someone slips."

Poor maid, getting dragged out of her well-deserved sleep at this hour. Eleanor sighed. But that was the way of it, and the butler wasn't going to stoop to such a menial task.

"Good night, Mr. Stanley."

"Good night, miss. I'm sorry to have startled you."

"And I, you," she said, taking a few steps before realizing she was leaving him in darkness.

"Shall I stay with the lamp until you—"

He lit one of the wall sconces. "No need, miss."

She took another few steps away, then turned back, amazed at the play of shadows on the wall. Each of his movements was projected onto the wall as a long, spindly figure, stretching all the way up to the ceiling.

She shuddered again.

"Did someone arrive late tonight, after everyone went to bed?" she asked, trying not to stare at his Wellies, which were still dry.

"Not that I'm aware of, miss, and I believe I am aware of most everyone's comings and goings," he said pointedly, looking at her.

"Yes, I'm sure you are. However, there is rainwater in the front hall leading to the main stairs. You may want the maid to see to that, as well."

"Thank you, miss." He didn't look happy about being told something was amiss in his well-run house.

"Good night again, Mr. Stanley." She made a hasty retreat, pleased to return to her bedroom, which was still filled with lamplight and heat from the coals.

Shucking off her damp slippers and her wrap, she climbed into bed and snuggled beneath the covers.

Only then did she begin to wonder again about hearing a horse outside in the storm. As she drifted off to sleep, Eleanor had the absurd notion it was William Kidd looking for his long-lost treasure.

GRAY WAS AMAZED TO see what Eleanor had figured out by herself, almost exactly replicating the protagonist, William Legrand's deciphering skills from Poe's story *The Gold Bug*. When they met before breakfast and she excitedly drew out her work for his inspection, he nearly grabbed her to him and hugged her.

However, he did not want her to think every time they were alone he would paw at her. Although, truthfully, taking her in his arms was the first thing he thought of each time he saw her.

"If we can determine the next most common letter," she proposed, "perhaps we can substitute it for the semi-colon characters in the puzzle."

Considering her suggestion, he nodded. But it would be easier to take the route of Poe's character, since Grayson knew it would lead to the puzzle's solution.

"We might more easily use the most common word in the English language, and I've used it twice in this sentence already."

She frowned, thinking a moment, then her lovely face broke out into an even lovelier smile. "The."

"Yes, I believe so. Fill it in and see if your *e*'s line up."

She checked, and they did. It seemed there were six instances of *the*. She clapped her hands, her eyes sparkling up at him.

"That was very clever of you, Grayson."

He felt like a fraud since she'd worked out her clue on her own, whereas he had simply followed the text of *The Gold Bug*. Still, it was getting them closer to the outing he had planned, one which had caused him to go out in the storm to set up the night before.

He simply shrugged, not accepting her praise, nor denying it.

Eleanor wrote in as many *t*'s and *h*'s as they'd deciphered, not only for the word *the*, but in other places. When this led them to guess other words, they filled out more in the puzzle.

By the time they had solved nearly all of it, the scent of the morning meal had permeated the library, since they'd left the door appropriately open.

"Shall we stop for breakfast with the Angsley family so as not to appear rude?" he asked.

Eleanor agreed at once, and he considered it a good morning's work. The puzzle wasn't too easy for her, nor bogglingly difficult as to make her lose heart. Moreover, she seemed simply happy.

It delighted him to be the cause of her pleasure.

Gray was surprised a few minutes later when Eleanor asked those gathered at the table, "Does anyone know of a late-night visitor?"

How could she know he'd braved yet another autumn storm to put more of his birthday gift to her in place?

Luckily, no one knew anything.

Then Phoebe spoke up. She'd been sending him curious looks ever since Eleanor had met with her the day before to ensure the girl's silence.

"I had a sewing lesson this morning with Mrs. O'Connor, and she would like both Eleanor *and* Grayson to go to her cottage today."

He didn't appreciate the way she emphasized linking their names together, especially when she followed it with a girlish giggle.

"Do you know what she wants?" he asked, keeping his tone entirely placid. "Is there anything my mother needs me to bring?"

"Only Eleanor," Phoebe repeated.

Gray felt the heat rise in his face as he lowered his gaze to study the black pudding on his plate as if the sausages were fascinating.

"That's fine," Eleanor said. "I am free to go directly after we eat. Are you, Grayson?"

It still seemed strange, even exciting, to hear her use his given name, especially in company, but no one else seemed to think anything of it.

In any case, within the half hour, they were walking companionably toward the old granary lodge.

"I wonder if we shall hear from Turvey House today. I hope so," she said.

If a messenger came, Grayson would try to intercept the man. After all, if a note arrived saying it was all right for Eleanor to leave, then his plans would be ruined. On the other hand, he didn't want her to be worried over Margaret if her illness had passed.

"Who knows?" was all he could say, hoping he didn't sound as if he didn't care.

Knocking at his mother's door, they waited only a few moments before it swung open. His mother paused and looked from him to Eleanor and back again, and then she sent them both a beaming smile.

What was she up to?

"Come in, my dears. Don't you two look well! Phoebe passed along my message. What a good girl she is."

"Good day, Mrs. O'Connor," Eleanor said politely, as they stepped inside.

"Did you need something?" he asked, always wondering if he could do something to make her life easier, although his mother rarely asked for anything.

"Actually, yes. I need those misplaced spectacles, or I need new ones. I was hoping you could help me look, or we could go into town and buy some new ones."

But why Eleanor?

Without waiting for him to ask, his mother added, "If we go into town, as I fear we must, I thought Miss Eleanor would enjoy an outing, too."

"Oh, I would," she said. "Thank you for thinking of me. Shall we walk or ride?"

Gray laughed at her enthusiasm. "Shall we look for your old eyeglasses first, Mum?"

Perhaps as she'd known would happen, searching had done them no good, and before they knew it, the three of them were walking to the main house so Eleanor could get her mantle and reticule, and so Grayson could borrow a carriage, as they deemed the weather too dodgy for walking.

"I'll ask Cook if she needs anything," his mother said and disappeared in a different direction.

By the time he had a comfortable covered wagon harnessed to two ponies, Eleanor was standing out front.

"Where is my mother?" he asked her.

She shrugged, looking delightful, but then everything she did was delightful. If he didn't get this expedition under way, they would lose another entire day of deciphering William Kidd's fictional message, and she might have to leave before they reached the treasure.

"I'll go find her," he promised. "Can you hold the reins?"

"Of course," she said, not waiting for assistance but climbing aboard the dickey beside him. She opened her gloved palms expectantly.

Placing the reins in her hands, he longed to also place a kiss on her lips. As it was, he couldn't help leaning close so he could speak softly against the shell of her ear.

"When we return, we'll go directly to the library. Agreed?"

"Agreed."

Instantly, his head was filled with recollections of what they'd last done in the library besides discuss codes and pirates. He had held her lush bottom in his hands.

Swallowing, his mouth went instantly dry, and his body tensed with anticipation of doing it again. As he drew back, her gaze dropped to his lips, and it took all his strength not to kiss her.

Climbing off the seat, he dashed through the front door, hoping his mother wasn't standing on ceremony and walking around to the servants' entrance rather than using the front door.

However, she was right before him in the foyer, standing close to Mr. Stanley, and they were deep in conversation.

She jumped back a step, startled when he entered.

"We're ready," Gray told her before nodding a greeting to the butler, who nodded back before turning on his heel and disappearing down the hall.

In a few minutes, they were underway, and Gray felt a sense of satisfaction being with the two ladies whom he most admired and, dare he say, loved.

For the first time, he had to acknowledge how at the mere thought of Eleanor, the emotion flowing through him was love. His greatest wish was to cherish her, please her, and make her smile.

ELEANOR

IT WAS NEARLY TWO hours later, Eleanor and Grayson left his mother at her cottage with a new pair of spectacles, which she had promised not to misplace. As they crossed the back lawn, Eleanor looked up at him while he looked down at her, and they nearly started to run, both eager to return to the puzzle at last.

Seated in the library, Eleanor drew out her copy of the puzzle, while Grayson retrieved the original.

"Truly," she remarked, "we are nearly done with the deciphering, yet we shall still need to figure out spacing and, perhaps, punctuation in order to make it legible."

"We'll see," he said, and they got to work.

After a few minutes, he asked her, "Why don't you read what we have?"

Why don't you kiss me? she nearly said, then focused on the paper in front of her.

"Very well." She smoothed it with her hands and read aloud, "'A good glass in the bishop's hostel in the devil's seat twenty-one degrees and thirteen minutes northeast and by north main branch seventh limb east side shoot from the left eye of the death's head a bee line from the tree through the shot fifty feet out.'"

Grayson leaned closer while she spoke, his broad shoulder pressing against hers. Perhaps it was his nearness, but the words together didn't make sense. If she glanced at him, he would read the desire in her gaze. Nevertheless, after a hesitation, she did exactly that.

The passion blazing in his eyes took her breath away.

Did her own, plain brown eyes appear to glow like his?

Inevitably, he bent down and claimed her mouth with warm, firm lips. It seemed an eternity since their last kiss. If they weren't seated side-by-side, she could imagine his arms going around her.

Still, he turned his body and cradled her face in his hands. Then tilting his head, he deepened the kiss. When his tongue sought and gained entrance between her lips, she moaned, her body beginning to sizzle with pleasurable tingling.

When he released her, she dragged in a deep breath to steady herself.

Where was she? What were they doing? Good God, the door was open!

All that and more flitted through her head, until he spoke.

"Let's try to break this up into sensical phrases."

What?

"Oh, the puzzle. Yes." With her heart beating double time from his proximity, she tried her best to focus.

"'A good glass in the bishop's hostel,'" she read again. "Is there a tavern nearby with that name? Perhaps 'a good glass' of ale is intended?"

"No," he said, looking pensive.

Suddenly, she realized how ridiculous she'd been.

"In any case, these instructions could be for anywhere in the world," she pointed out. "It was silly for me to think even for an instant that Captain Kidd had ever been here in Bedfordshire."

His expression came over shocked.

Quietly and deadly serious, he whispered to her. "I assumed you knew."

The hair on the back of her neck raised in alarm at his tone.

CHAPTER ELEVEN

Eleanor swallowed. "Knew what?"

Grayson sat back, crossing his arms over his broad chest.

"Local lore has always held that the pirate came back from one of his journeys before he went back to the colonies, and that he sailed as far as he could up the River Severn to Gloucester, and then was going overland to Dundee for one last visit home to Scotland."

Eleanor thought for a moment. "He was going to Dundee by way of Bedford? Why on earth would he detour inland so far?"

Grayson shook his head, his lustrous, raven-black hair moving softly.

"Then you really haven't ever heard our stories?"

"No," she confessed.

"Why didn't Beryl ever tell you?"

"I don't know," she said, becoming excited by his tone. "Or John, for that matter."

Grayson nodded. "I don't think Cam ever believed the tale of Captain Kidd coming to Bedfordshire, so that's no matter, but we've found proof he did, haven't we? The so-called bishop's hostel is just a big rock down by the river. And Kidd came this way because he was traveling with one of his pirate mates who lived in Brayfield, just down the road. They were going to pay off the man's family, as pirates do."

"Do they?" She had no knowledge of what pirates did, but maybe Grayson knew this from Beryl's husband.

"Well, they did," he insisted. "Legend has it they reached the River Great Ouse east of here, around Buckingham, and came all this way on a raft."

"A raft?" Eleanor tried to picture a fierce pirate on a raft.

"It's just the way the story goes, but they came with plenty of treasure. Unfortunately for them, some local man figured out who they were, and the sheriff was notified. Rumor has it they quickly buried whatever jewels and coins they had with them somewhere hereabouts. Then, instead of going to Dundee, which might have been expected, they left for America."

He stared deeply into her eyes. "You know how it ended for the miserable pirate?"

She nodded, fascinated by the husky tone of his voice. A chill raced down her spine at the notion of the pirate having once been so close to Angsley Hall, even if it was a hundred and fifty years earlier.

Grayson continued, "Kidd was eventually captured and imprisoned in Boston before being sent back to England," he paused a moment, then added, "for execution."

Every child knew the story of how the rope broke the first time they tried to hang Captain Kidd, and how the executioner had to re-hang the pirate.

How awful! Eleanor imagined it would make for an angry ghost if ghosts were real. She had never believed in them, which was why reading Gothic novels didn't bother her. Not only did she love to be thrilled and terrified, she liked how the narrator explained all the mysterious things, often with wind banging a door or rattling a shutter.

"And you know where this rock is?" Eleanor asked, staring at him, realizing she enjoyed simply looking at his fine features.

"You're gaping at me," he said.

"Am I?" She supposed her mouth had dropped open a little while she was admiring him.

He grinned. "That's fine. I like when you look at me that way."

She smiled back, then reminded him, "The rock?"

"Yes. I can take you there if you like. It's not far from the tree we climbed."

"We should figure out more before we go on an expedition. And we should take supplies."

"Like a canteen of brandy?" he proposed.

She laughed. "No. Like shovels and picks. Maybe even a compass."

"Good idea, but as you said, let's figure out more."

He seemed to be waiting for her to study the paper again, so she did, although Eleanor much preferred, at that moment, to look at him.

"If it's a rock and not a tavern, then the glass must be other than one for drinking. A looking glass, for instance."

"Also, not a very practical thing to take to a rock."

"True." She could think of nothing else.

"It must be some type of glass a pirate uses," Grayson surmised, tapping his chin.

The word jumped suddenly into her mind. "A spyglass. You know, a telescope. That would be a useful thing to take to a rock, especially if one were then looking for something particular, such as treasure."

Grayson rubbed his hands together. "I think you're on to something. Pirates, all sailors for that matter, always have a spyglass, don't they?"

Leaning close again, he read further. "I can help with the next part. The devil's seat is another local term for a section of the bishop's hostel rock that seems almost as if it were carved for sitting upon."

Eleanor shook her head. "I can hardly believe Beryl never took me to the rock or mentioned such a thing as a devil's seat."

"Don't be too hard on her. You are far more of the nature dweller than she is. She may never have climbed the rock in her whole life."

Eleanor shrugged. She would let it go for now, but it seemed strange indeed her best friend had not mentioned Captain Kidd once, even after Beryl fell in love with her own pirate.

"I assume the rest of the numbers and directions tell us which way to point the telescope," she surmised. "And thus, we will need a compass after all. I hope you can handle all that particular stuff. I am not keen on numbers and degrees and directions."

He nodded solemnly. "I believe I can handle that."

With sheer excitement, Eleanor clapped her hands spontaneously, then hoped he didn't think her childish.

"I don't believe we can go further with this puzzle," she said, "not without going to the rock and sitting on the devil's seat." *Even the very words were thrilling.*

He nodded. "Apparently, we shall see a tree with at least seven branches."

She mused a moment. "Trees change a lot in one hundred and fifty years."

His eyes widened. "Yes, I hadn't thought of that. However, if it is a big tree, then perhaps it will be easy to figure out. The branch will simply be longer and thicker."

"But as the tree has grown, the branch will have moved upward, will it not?"

Grayson made a sound of exasperation, but he only shrugged.

"It will make no matter. Our coordinates will still be the same. We may simply have to look up higher than expected. It says we're looking for a death's head. How many of those can there be in a tree?"

She shivered again. "Hopefully not too many!"

He stood, reached for her hand, and drew her to stand beside him.

"I shall keep you safe."

They were standing too close, and the library door was agape.

"When shall we go?" she asked, staring up at him, ready for anything, as long as they were together in this adventure. "Is it far?"

He didn't answer. He was staring at her mouth.

"Grayson? Is it far?"

His gaze rose to hers.

"Is what far?"

"Don't tease me," she scolded.

"All right." He winked at her, and something inside her did a strange twitch. "We have to go by foot as there is no road or even cart path wide enough. I hate to say it, but since my mother's excursion took up the day and the light is waning, we ought to find a spyglass and the rest of the supplies today and start early tomorrow. Maybe we could pack a picnic to eat at the bishop's hostel."

"That's a grand idea. And so we are prepared, how do you propose we shoot something from the skull's left eye?"

He considered. "We could let gravity do its work and simply drop something straight down to mark the spot."

"Very well. Then we need some twine or…," she paused and clapped her hands again. "Yarn. Lady Angsley knits and does needlework. She must have tons of spun wool."

"No need to bother her," he said. "I'll get a rope or string. In fact, if you can arrange a picnic, I'll get everything else."

"How shall we transport it all?"

"Don't you worry, Miss Eleanor. I shall amaze you with what I can scare up. By tomorrow, you shall be on the devil's seat, searching for a death's head."

She had to contain a squeal of sheer delight.

It was a Gothic novel come to life, and even better with Grayson as her companion in mystery.

THEIR PLANS FELL APART entirely just before dinner. When the Angsleys, along with Grayson and Eleanor, were gathered in the drawing room, a messenger came from Turvey House.

Lord Angsley read it, then looked up with a smile. "Good news. John is entirely recovered, and Lady Margaret is…"

When he hesitated, Gray felt Eleanor tense with worry even though she was seated across the drawing room from him.

"How is she?" Eleanor prompted.

Lord Angsley looked at her. "They had the physician there. With his determination and with how she has been since then, they have decided Lady Margaret is not ill at all but rather," he paused again, looking around the room.

"What is it, dear?" Lady Angsley asked.

"I am not sure I should discuss it with you and the children and others of the weaker sex present." He looked toward Eleanor.

"For pity's sake," his wife exclaimed, "we are all family, and as one of the 'weaker sex,' I can tell you, there isn't much I cannot handle."

"Very well, my love. The news is that Lady Margaret is with child."

A universal gasp went up around the room. A weight lifted off Gray's shoulders on behalf of his best friend. Cam would have gone mad if anything had been seriously wrong with his wife. Not to mention the terrible pain it would have caused Eleanor and the rest of the Blackwoods.

However, one thing didn't make sense. "If Margaret was never ill, then why was Cam feverish and sick to his stomach, as well?"

Lord Angsley chuckled, and his wife joined in. Her ladyship answered.

"Sometimes, when a couple is very much in love," she paused to exchange a glance with her husband, "the father-to-be shares symptoms with the mother-to-be. It is common."

Eleanor shook her head in wonder, making a wry face at Gray. He grinned back at her. Then the ramifications hit him.

"Did they say anything else?"

"Only that they are looking forward to Eleanor's visit now more than ever, and she should head there directly tomorrow after breakfast."

He wanted to yell. All his plans were in tatters. Her face paled, in fact, as she stared at him. Undoubtedly, they were both thinking of their much-anticipated adventure, yet perhaps for different reasons. She had no idea what he had waiting for her at the end of it.

On the bright side, he would be accompanying her home. Their association would continue unbroken, but he knew Eleanor's mind. She would start to ask others about the Captain Kidd legend as it pertained to Bedfordshire. More than one person would happily tell her she was laboring under severe misinformation and that the pirate was never in this area.

Then what? He would have to tell her the truth and entirely ruin the surprise.

Yet, perhaps he could gain them one last day.

"Miss Blackwood and I had decided to go on a picnic tomorrow. Perhaps we could delay our return," he said as casually as he could.

"Nonsense," Lord Angsley said. "The sisters must wish to be reunited as soon as possible."

But Lady Angsley arched her eyebrow questioningly, and Gray believed he might have an ally in the lady of the manor.

"I'm sure everyone will still be delighted to see Eleanor at Turvey House whether it is tomorrow or the day after."

Did Lady Angsley just wink at him?

"Besides," Eleanor said. "It wasn't merely a picnic."

Oh dear, what was she going to say? Hopefully nothing about Captain Kidd.

"We were going sightseeing."

Phoebe laughed. "What is there to see here?"

Eleanor looked at him, and he shook his head.

"There is plenty to see here," Lord Angsley assured everyone. "There is the castle."

"They've torn down nearly all of it," Phoebe argued with her father. "Last year, they even destroyed the last parts of the barbican to make room for more cottages."

"The motte still exists," his lordship said less enthusiastically. "There's also St. Paul's."

"Father, it's hardly St. Paul's in London, is it? It's just a church, not a cathedral." This came from Asher, who hardly ever said a word.

Gray wondered how Lord Angsley would take to being corrected by his eldest son, who was only twelve.

Apparently delighted Asher had spoken at all, his lordship beamed at him. "You're right, hardly a cathedral, my boy. However, Eleanor hasn't seen the chapel or the stained glass, so that's something."

"They both sound very interesting," Eleanor said, although she had, indeed, seen both with Beryl more than once over the years.

Bless her, Gray thought. They would see their adventure through after all.

THE MORNING'S HEAVY RAIN was a bitter disappointment.

"Should we leave for Turvey House?" Eleanor wondered, standing with Grayson, looking out the back of the house onto the terrace. "Since we cannot go on our treasure hunt or a picnic."

She held the telescope they had borrowed from Lord Angsley up to her eye, surveying the landscape.

She felt Grayson shrug, his large shoulder moving beside her.

"I see no point in travelling," he said.

"Maybe we should put on capes and Wellies and go find the bishop's hostel anyway."

"Too slippery," he said. "Are you willing to wait until it clears up? Or are you eager to get to your sister's?"

"Oh, dear," she said. "Both, I suppose."

He chuckled at her silly answer.

Then her attention was wrested by movement by the old granary lodge. She could clearly see all the doors through the spyglass and, plainly, the Angsley butler had just come out of Mrs. O'Connor's rooms.

What was he doing there so early?

"What do you make of that?" Eleanor muttered, recalling encountering the butler coming in early her first morning at the manor.

"What is it?" he asked, peering through the windowpane beside her.

She wished she had said nothing. It wasn't her business, nor really Grayson's, for that matter.

Taking a deep breath, she tried to distract him without lying.

"Let's go have coffee."

He stared at her. Then, his hand shot out, and he snatched the spyglass from her.

"Let me see," he said belatedly, setting it to his right eye and looking out.

"That wasn't nice," she said, nudging him so he couldn't see properly, then she reached up and tried to take it back.

He thwarted her by hunching his back and turning away so he could look out while preventing her from reaching the spyglass.

"I see Mr. Stanley walking across the pasture." Grayson scanned the rest of the view, right to left and back. "Nothing else."

Lowering it, he looked at her. "What did you see?"

Mutinously, she stared up at him.

"Tell me," he demanded.

She shook her head.

Minimizing and then pocketing the telescope, he reached out and, to her surprise, he tickled her.

"Tell me."

She squealed and tried to get away, but he held her fast. His fingers were prodding her, trying to find her tender spot, creeping up her rib cage. She squirmed against him and, in doing so, his hands brushed the sides of her breasts, taking her breath away.

They froze, and it was as if the world fell away, leaving them alone in the gray light of the back hallway.

Their gazes locked.

"Eleanor," he said softly, turning her name into a caress.

"Yes?" *Was this the moment he would declare his feelings for her?*

CHAPTER TWELVE

"Tell me what you saw," Grayson ordered again, then he cracked a smile and found her ticklish area under her ribs, making her squirm.

Eleanor shrieked and truly couldn't catch her breath. Eventually, she nodded, and he halted.

"I saw Mr. Stanley, just like you," she told him.

"And?"

When she paused, he took hold of her again, preparing to tickle her mercilessly once more.

"He came from your mother's doorway."

"What?" He released her, frowned down at her, then glanced back out the window. "He's nearly here! Quick, out of sight."

Taking her hand, he half dragged her down the hallway to the deserted drawing room. Pulling her inside, he closed the door behind them.

"I wouldn't want him to think he was being spied on."

"Even if he was," she pointed out.

"When you asked, *what do you make of it?* I know what *you* made of it. My mother and Mr. Stanley! Can it be?"

"They've both worked here a long time, and they are both without spouses. There's nothing wrong with it," she hesitated, "unless you do not approve."

"Why wouldn't I?" he asked.

"I don't know. For me, it was simply surprising. He popped out of the doorway, and I reacted."

"Should I ask her?"

Eleanor scrunched up her nose, imagining such a conversation between mother and son. "You might embarrass her."

"True." He paused. "All these years, I've never seen her courted by Mr. Stanley or even keep company with anyone. I suppose with them both living under the same roof..." He shook his head to clear his thoughts.

"Perhaps that's why your mother doesn't wish to go to Turvey House and live with you there."

"That would explain it. Do you really want coffee?"

"No. I am thinking if Mr. Stanley can venture out in this, why can't we? Let us, at least, take a walk."

Tilting his head, he considered her proposal.

"All right. Cloaks and Wellingtons are in order."

The scampering of feet on the stairs alerted them to company. Asher's head came around the open door a moment later.

"What are you doing?"

The poor lad had seemed deflated ever since Philip left.

"We are taking a walk in the rain. Would you like to come?" she asked him.

The boy's face broke out in a smile, and even though she would lose the opportunity to be alone with Grayson and perhaps be kissed by him, it seemed she'd done a good deed.

"Shall we look for bugs?" he asked.

She grinned at Grayson, who nodded.

"Yes," she said. "In fact, there is one in particular we hope to find. A gold one."

ELEANOR

AN HOUR AND A half later, Eleanor came indoors to a delicious hot breakfast of kippers and eggs, with toast and bacon. She ate heartily, noticing Grayson and Asher did the same. Something about a long country walk gave one an appetite, even if no rock or tree climbing was involved.

Instead, there had been plenty of looking at the underside of leaves and scrabbling around amongst wild roses, as well as discovering all manner of other wildflowers. Plenty of bugs had been collected in a jar Asher brought, but no gold beetle.

As she finished her breakfast, Mr. Stanley entered the room.

After seeing him earlier that morning and catching him unaware, she felt as if she'd intruded upon his private life. The warmth bloomed in her cheeks as he approached her.

"Miss Eleanor," he said, bowing slightly. "Mrs. O'Connor would like you to go visit her when you are otherwise unoccupied."

She was surprised at him mentioning Grayson's mother since her mind was filled with the possibility the butler and Mrs. O'Connor were having a relationship.

He paused, standing beside her chair, glancing at her empty plate. She took that to mean Mr. Stanley considered her to be unoccupied at that very instant.

Pushing out her chair, Eleanor rose to her feet. The males at the table, including Lord Angsley stood, too.

"Please, be seated," she said. "I am a fast eater, which is a terrible habit, I know, and possibly bad for my digestion. In any case, I shall see you all later."

With a backward glance at Grayson, who made a questioning face, to which she responded with a lift of her shoulder, she left.

The rain had barely let up, so she donned a dry cloak and her trusty Wellies and snatched up an umbrella by the door, before venturing outside once more. In five minutes, she was knocking on Mrs. O'Connor's door.

It flew open as if the woman had been waiting for her, perhaps watching out the window.

"Thank you for coming, dear girl. Would you care for tea?" she asked, wearing a decidedly worried expression.

"No, thank you. I just came from breakfast," Eleanor said, looking at Mrs. O'Connor with new eyes. "*Mr. Stanley* said you wished to see me."

She waited for a reaction to his name, but the woman's countenance didn't alter. So, Eleanor asked, "Is there something I can do for you?"

Mrs. O'Connor hesitated as if still wrestling with herself over whether to speak her mind. Then she dropped into the closest chair.

Eleanor wasn't sure what else to do, so she sat, as well.

Grayson's mother placed her hands on the table, and they were clearly trembling.

Eleanor's sympathy went out to the woman, whatever she was dealing with. Perhaps she was in love with Mr. Stanley, and he had broken her heart.

Placing her hands over Mrs. O'Connor's, Eleanor said, "You may confide in me if it will help. I know how to keep my own counsel."

The woman's gaze flew to hers, and her eyes shone with sadness.

"I have a dreadful secret."

Eleanor nodded calmly, although her heart had started to beat faster. *Why would Mrs. O'Connor invite her to the lodge to hear her secret? Unless...*

"Is it to do with Grayson?"

After another moment's hesitation, Mrs. O'Connor nodded.

"I have made some fine needlepoint in my day. I've even made lace, a time-consuming task if ever there was one. And I've sewn hundreds of dresses. But Gray is my best work. He is a good son and a good man."

She paused, and then in a whispered voice, she added, "He means the world to me."

Eleanor gently squeezed the woman's hands. *Did Mrs. O'Connor know how much she admired her son, too?*

"I expect you're wondering why I'm telling you," Gray's mother said as if reading Eleanor's thoughts. "I've seen you together a few times recently, but also over the years, and you've grown into a lovely young lady, one whom my son cannot keep his eyes off of."

Eleanor felt the heat rush into her cheeks.

"I have something I want to tell Gray, but not while I'm alive."

Eleanor gasped. *What could she mean?*

"Are you ill?" Knowing how Grayson doted on his mother, it would devastate him to lose her unexpectedly.

"No, dear. I'm quite fit except for my eyes." The woman withdrew her hands from under Eleanor's and pointed to the glasses also on the table. "I shall not lose them again. Or, I may do, actually, because I'm not used to caring for them, but I'll try not to."

"Why don't you want to tell Grayson your secret until after you're gone?"

Mrs. O'Connor hung her head. "I don't want him to think ill of me, and this information will change his life a little . . . or perhaps, a lot. I'm not sure, but it could." His mother frowned and added, "There are greater ramifications, others are involved."

Then she gave a little groan. "While it is only in here," Mrs. O'Connor continued, tapping her head, "it is a small matter, of no consequence to anyone, harming no one. But once it is out here," she said, gesturing to the room in general, "then it is a huge matter. At least to some."

"Naturally, you would prefer not to deal with it?" Eleanor guessed.

Mrs. O'Connor sighed. "I would prefer no one had to deal with it. And I believe some secrets should never be told, especially if they do no good to anybody in the telling, and mayhap only harm. But this one, eventually, should be told, at least to Gray."

Eleanor pondered a moment. "If that is the case, and you truly wish for the truth to remain hidden away for now, why not write your message on a piece of paper and set it aside with instructions for it to be read upon your passing."

There, that seemed a sensible notion. Eleanor was pleased with herself for thinking of it.

"I can't write," the woman explained, a small catch in her voice betraying her emotion. "Nor read, of course. I have no way of documenting what I want to tell Gray after I'm gone."

Drats! Eleanor hadn't considered that.

"However, I have considered doing exactly what you're suggesting, creating a last testament, except instead of worldly possessions to give him, I have only my secret. I merely need someone to write it for me."

She gave Eleanor a beseeching look and a plaintive smile.

"But you're young yet," Eleanor protested, not thinking herself the correct vessel for Mrs. O'Connor's confidences. "Moreover, if there is something important you want to impart, surely it would be better for you to do so while your son can still speak with you about it. Perhaps he'll have questions."

"I can put all the answers on the page better than I can say them." Her voice had fallen to a whisper. "While I'm still here and can look in his eyes, I don't want him to blame me, nor do I want him to do anything rash."

Eleanor nodded. "Truly, you think your secret might incite him to rash action?"

"My Gray is a good man," she repeated, then fell silent a moment as Eleanor waited. "I think you agree with me on this."

They locked gazes, until Eleanor, not wishing to lie, simply nodded. After all, there could be no harm in letting Mrs. O'Connor know she believed Grayson to be the most appealing man in the world.

"When learning the truth, he might behave strangely or out of character, at least until he settles in with it," his mother added. "He might be angry or feel jealous."

Settle in with it? Eleanor thought that a strange way of discussing the truth.

Moreover, she could hardly imagine anything causing Grayson to be angry or jealous. However, this wasn't a riddle for an evening's entertainment. This was something serious, and Eleanor wished she could ask Jenny or Maggie or her own mother what to do.

"Very well," she said at last. "If you think you cannot tell him, I'll write down whatever you wish."

"You will have to swear to keep it secret and never tell a living soul."

When his mother said it like that, it sounded ominous. Eleanor obviously couldn't tell a *dead* soul. *And what of Grayson?* They were forming a wonderful bond. She felt closer to him every day. Her youthful obsession with the handsome man had blossomed into genuine feelings of . . . love.

Dare she say the words, even to herself? *I love him.*

How could she swear to withhold an important secret from him, only to reveal on his mother's deathbed that she knew it all along?

"I can see you're struggling with this," Mrs. O'Connor said. "And it's because you have feelings for my boy. I can see it on your face when you look at him. And it's plain to see he cares for you, as well."

His mother sighed. "Since the day he was born, I have kept this from him. I know how hard it is to lie to one you love with all your heart. I won't ask it of you."

"Then what shall we do?" Eleanor felt desperately torn. She wanted to help Mrs. O'Connor, who looked all but crushed. And curiosity burned in her to know the dreadful secret but not at the expense of her own peace of mind. For once she learned it, she wouldn't be able to look Grayson in the eyes without feeling guilty.

No, she must not be told, Eleanor decided. She wasn't strong enough to carry such a burden without blurting it out to him at some point.

Then, all at once, an idea hit her.

"I could teach you to write."

"Never," Mrs. O'Connor said. Then the next instant, she asked, "Could you?"

"Yes, why not?" Eleanor clapped her hands with excitement. "You simply need to keep your spectacles handy."

She was rewarded with a smile. "If I could get the words on paper, then I would feel as if I'd done my duty as his mother."

Almost wanting to cry with relief, Eleanor watched as Grayson's mother warmed to the idea. Nodding to herself, Mrs. O'Connor said, "I think I could do this."

"Why, positively you can! We shall start at once. We need only some paper and a pen. And maybe a few books so you see how words work. I shall go to Lord Angsley's library and get everything we need."

She rose and hurried to the door when Mrs. O'Connor stopped her.

"I understand you've had word from the Earl of Cambrey. Your sister is doing better, isn't she?"

"Yes, she is. I shall be . . . Oh." Eleanor realized the problem. "I shall be leaving soon. I was supposed to go today. We delayed leaving because Grayson and I had a picnic planned but for the rain."

Mrs. O'Connor nodded, looking a little crestfallen. "I suppose we shall have to wait until the next time Miss Beryl returns and you come to visit her."

Eleanor frowned. She hated to let Grayson's mother down. This was important, perhaps one of the truly useful things she'd ever been called upon to do in her young life.

"My sister is not ill and never was, so there is no rush for me to be by her side. She is carrying a child, as it turns out.

If the Angsleys don't mind my staying, then I shall teach you."

"Oh dear," Mrs. O'Connor said, looking uncertain.

"Truly, it is no trouble. We shall start by having you practice writing individual letters. Then I am confident within a few days, maybe a week, I can teach you enough to sound out your words so you can write something legible, although most likely not perfect."

"I am only concerned what you will tell the lord and lady. I never brought up not being able to read and write. No one ever asked, and I never needed such skills. I wouldn't want them to think I haven't got a brain in my head."

"You have made lace," she reminded Grayson's mother, "and hundreds of dresses, which undeniably fit her ladyship and the other Angsley girls perfectly."

"Yes," she said, looking surer of herself. Then she frowned. "Still, it wouldn't do for them to think you've stayed here for my sake."

"Do not worry. I won't embarrass you. I'll think of something. Are you ready to start today?"

Mrs. O'Connor stood and closed the few steps between them. "Yes, I am." Then she hugged her "And I thank you, Miss Eleanor. Truly, I do. I'm glad you and my boy have feelings for one another."

Eleanor couldn't speak for the lump in her throat, so she nodded and slipped out the door.

GRAYSON WAS HALF READING, half watching out of the back windows of the morning room, awaiting Eleanor's return. When he finally saw her dashing across the lawn in the rain, he intercepted her at the terrace before ushering her inside and taking her wet cloak and the umbrella from her.

"Is everything all right?"

"Yes," she said, but she didn't look him in the eyes.

"What did my mother want to speak with you about?"

Eleanor shrugged, before sitting and taking a long time to remove her Wellington boots. Her slippers were beneath the seat where she had left them.

For a moment, he got to see her stockinged feet, and in that brief time, his brain seemed to empty. He watched her slip each of her slender feet into a cream-colored kidskin shoe, useless for anything except staying indoors.

From what he could see, her feet were shaped perfectly, with a delicate arch to the underside, which his fingers itched to stroke.

The notion of seeing those same feet unclothed and of touching her sweet toes enflamed him as much as watching one of his London ladies remove her entire corset.

"Grayson?"

He was still staring at her soft shoes when her voice brought his gaze upward. She was now standing.

"Have you seen Lady Angsley? Is she on this floor?"

"I think she is with Phoebe in her ladyship's upstairs sitting room," he told her.

"Thank you. I will see you later. It is nearly time for lunch, isn't it?"

She smiled at him and walked down the hall toward the main staircase.

"Eleanor," he called after her.

She paused and turned to him.

"My mother?"

"Oh, she is fine. We just had a cup of gossip-water. You know how women can be. Interestingly enough, she already knew about the missive from Turvey House. Perhaps a bird told her, a tall, butler-shaped bird."

"Indeed. Are we going to . . . to do something together?" He cringed at his own lame question. *What a dunce, he sounded!* But she seemed preoccupied and a little indifferent.

"Yes," she said, and his misgiving lifted. "Later."

With that, she left him. *Later? When?*

Unfortunately, at the midday meal, his favorite female was absent.

"Where is Eleanor?" he asked to one and all.

Lady Angsley answered since her husband was preparing for a visit to London. The queen summoned Lord Angsley at a moment's notice when she needed her Spanish ambassador, and apparently, she needed him the next day.

"Eleanor is at the granary lodge."

"No," he corrected her, "she went there earlier."

Lady Angsley nodded and sipped her tea. "She's there again, as far as I know."

What on earth was going on at the lodge? He was going to get to the bottom of it as soon as he finished his meal.

Unfortunately, he had to wait for her ladyship and the others to finish, too, as without Lord Angsley present, and with no real reason for abandoning the table, it would have been terribly rude for him to make himself scarce. It wasn't like at breakfast, when everyone was loosey-goosey.

Cooling his heels, letting his mind wander as he drank a cold glass of ale and idly pushed the remainder of a potato around his plate on the end of his fork, Gray considered how Mr. Stanley had gone to his mother's and given her the news from Turvey House.

Had that been the butler's main purpose for visiting her? And why? He considered the day before when he'd caught them in close quarters talking in the front hall.

When he finally got out of the dining room, he was going to get some answers.

CHAPTER THIRTEEN

Eleanor looked on proudly as Mrs. O'Connor copied the twenty-six letters in front of her. The best place to start their grand task, it had seemed to them both, was for the older woman to practice writing, even if the letters were nothing more than mysterious symbols. In fact, the alphabet was as perplexing to Grayson's mother as Captain Kidd's puzzle had first been to Eleanor.

After she had spoken privately to Lady Angsley, telling her as little as possible, she'd returned to the lodge with her supplies. Luckily, Lord Angsley had been in his private study preparing for a trip, making it easy for Eleanor to enter the library and secure some paper, pens, and books.

It had been a little more difficult to avoid Grayson, but doing so was a must, for he would be full of questions.

To that deceitful end, Eleanor told Asher how Mr. O'Connor enjoyed a good ride, especially on a cloudy day, sending the boy to find him. Since the rain had let up, she had no doubt Grayson would indulge the young Angsley lad.

While Eleanor had started her lesson with letters and sounds, she and Mrs. O'Connor had eaten a light repast.

Around some thickly sliced bread and butter, cheese, and pickled onions, she'd pointed to letters in a book, before writing them in alphabetical order on the paper.

With Mrs. O'Connor having copied and re-copied the letters thrice, they were ready to sound out vowels. In another half hour, the woman had also written *to, as,* and *no.*

Perhaps not the most useful words to start with, Eleanor thought. Then she recalled the most used word, *the,* and explained about the "th" sound.

Mrs. O'Connor dutifully wrote *the.*

"You're doing very well," Eleanor praised. It was easier than she'd anticipated. Certainly, nothing like teaching a child who had so many other things to learn. Grayson's mother could focus and had a sharp memory.

"Let me know when you grow weary," Eleanor told her.

"I'm too excited to be tired," Mrs. O'Connor exclaimed. "I know you said there are double vowel words, too, with *o*'s and *u*'s put together, but I think I would like to stick to the simpler spellings today."

Eleanor agreed with her, and they continued sounding out such words as *hat, cat, dog,* and even *plate* with its tricky silent *e.* Then she realized how difficult English truly was when she considered explaining how many ways a *y* could be spoken, and how many other letters, especially in combination, such as *ee* and *ie,* could sound exactly the same. And then there was the puzzling word *you.*

Undeniably, it would be easier if she knew the nature of the secret, for then she could teach Mrs. O'Connor those words in particular. Of course, that would defeat the whole purpose of Eleanor not learning the woman's private business, nor having to hide it from Grayson.

A knock at the door followed by the rattling of the handle brought them both to their feet. They had planned for this. Firstly, they had locked the door, something Mrs. O'Connor normally only did at night. Secondly, Eleanor was prepared to snatch up the two books and papers she'd brought and run into the other room to shove them under the bed.

At the same time, Grayson's mother unfolded a complicated lace piece she hadn't worked on for years and, as Eleanor returned to her seat, Mrs. O'Connor had laid it across the table and was already unlocking the door.

"Hello, my boy. I don't know how that got locked." Mrs. O'Connor was the embodiment of calm, answering his unspoken question even as he greeted them both.

Seeing Grayson's concerned expression, however, caused Eleanor to feel quite the opposite. Instead of placid, she was anxious. She would have to pretend to be doing lacework, and she feared if he looked deeply into her eyes, he would see her deception.

"How was your ride?" she asked to break the silence.

Instantly, she knew she'd said the wrong thing.

"How did you know I went riding?"

She would have to start prevaricating immediately, something she loathed doing, especially with Grayson.

"I saw you through the window. Weren't you with another rider?"

"Yes," he said, still looking at her strangely. "With Asher. The boy is a natural horseman."

When she did nothing more than offer him a smile, Grayson seemed to relax. He took a seat as his mother cleaned up "their little project," as she called it, and put on the kettle for tea.

Luckily, Eleanor didn't have to figure out a single strand of weaving lace. She relaxed then, too, and listened to Grayson tell them where he took Asher and how he taught the boy to canter evenly and levelly.

Mrs. O'Connor brought out the tin of biscuits.

"We should discuss when you want to leave," Grayson said, "and give Lady Angsley some notice. Lord Angsley leaves tomorrow. Perhaps we should do the same."

Surprised, since Eleanor assumed he would want to stay as long as possible in order to see their treasure hunt through to the end, she glanced at Mrs. O'Connor.

The woman's face was emotionless as they'd already discussed this very matter. Indeed, Eleanor had talked with Lady Angsley earlier about an extended stay while she worked on something with Grayson's mother. When her ladyship had pressed the matter, Eleanor had told a small lie about wanting to learn to make lace as a present for her own mother.

Dear God, don't punish me for lying, she prayed, while knowing in her bones it was a sin.

Lady Angsley, a little nonplussed but agreeable all the same, approved the extended stay at once.

"I would very much like to stay longer," Eleanor told Grayson. "Your mother and I were just getting started."

He stared at the pile of lace on the chair. Then he frowned. "I thought you hated needle work."

Eleanor opened her mouth, then closed it. *This was the problem with lying,* she realized. *One eventually got caught.*

"Making lace is not needle work, my boy," Mrs. O'Connor said with conviction, as if he were a dunce to confuse the two.

"In any case," Eleanor added, "we can try our *picnic* again in the morning, perhaps?"

"Very well." He winked at her, apparently pleased to have another day for their adventure if the weather cooperated. Then he twisted his mouth with displeasure.

"Mum, I think we should get some biscuits from the Angsleys' new cook. These are inferior to anything they have at the hall."

"Bring me some next time, then," Mrs. O'Connor said. "You are a wonderful son."

THE NEXT MORNING WAS sunny, and Eleanor rejoiced as she tossed the covers back and hurried to dress. She knew Grayson would be ready and waiting.

"There's my adventurous girl," he said as she hurried into the library. "I can't think many females would be eager to jump up early out of a soft bed for an outdoor adventure."

Warming down to her toes at his praise, she said, "More than you think, I would warrant."

In truth, however, she didn't know any other women who quite enjoyed the natural world as she did, nor who would grow gleeful over climbing a rock.

"I have only encountered those who wouldn't dare get their dresses torn or dirty," Grayson confessed, "or their gloves soiled or their hair knotted, for that matter."

Eleanor knew those women. They were the ones during the Season who never had a hair out of place, not even at a boating event. They were too perfect.

But she was the one standing next to the deliciously handsome Grayson O'Connor!

She beamed at him.

"Do you have our supplies?"

"Yes, nearby," he said, tucking one of her errant locks behind her ear. She shivered at his touch. "And the picnic?" he asked.

She hadn't ordered one from the kitchen staff the night before in case it had turned into another day of rain.

"In the twirl of a pig's tail," she promised. "By the time you have everything in a wagon outside, I will meet you with a basket of goodies."

True to her word, Eleanor found Grayson dragging a small cart, with a shovel, a pickaxe, some rope and string, a lantern, and a sack, which she assumed contained the spyglass and compass.

She placed their basket of food in the cart, as well. Then, clapping her hands, she could hardly stop herself from running on ahead.

"Finally, we are on our quest, and not for a silly gold beetle either."

"There is no one I would rather be questing with than you, Miss Eleanor."

"Nor I," she confessed. "Look how glorious it is when the sun shines. I believe we appreciate it here more than anywhere else in the world for the sheer scarcity of bright British sunshine."

"You may be right," he said. "If I'm going to be in constant rain, however, I'm happier here than in London."

She scrunched up her face at the thought. Heavy rain in Town was a nightmare, with the streets turning to rivers of muddy water and stinking sewage. And even when it rained, the Season continued with the added nuisance of dragging sodden, filthy hems around the dancefloor if one were unlucky enough to have been splashed on the way inside. Not to mention the slippery tiles!

Wellies would be useful sometimes on the ballroom floor. She imagined them poking out from under one of her evening gowns.

"What has you smiling so broadly?" he asked.

"The sheer joy of being alive and here with you. And for my Wellies and my straw hat, too."

"Indeed," he said, "you are blessed with an abundance of riches. We both are."

In companionable silence, they trekked over the pasture. They did not go down the same path to the river which they'd gone before and which she'd traversed many times over the years. Instead, after another few minutes walking parallel to the Ouse, Grayson pointed out a large birch.

"This marks the path to the rock," he said, and they finally turned into the trees.

It wasn't such a broad or clear-cut path as the other one, but it was easy to follow. She noted how some of it looked as if it had recently been cleared, for the ends of small branches and twigs were fresh and green.

Except for the sound of the still-dripping leaves, the only noise was from the occasional bird, and in the distance, the sound of the swollen River Great Ouse rushing along its full bed.

"Are we there yet? Are we close?" she asked after a few hundred feet as Grayson pushed aside a low-hanging branch and let her pass before he and the wagon followed.

"Nearly. The journey is half the fun, though, isn't it?"

"True, but I have been dreaming of seeing the bishop's hostel for many days now. You cannot blame me for being eager."

Another twenty yards or so and there was a glade with a towering boulder that must have been moved there eons ago by an ice flow.

"Look at it!" she exclaimed. "It's magnificent."

His gentle laughter filled her ears despite the river being loud.

"I never considered this rock to be magnificent," he said, "but I will from now on."

"Have you climbed it many times?" She started to circle the giant sarsen, trailing her gloved hand on its craggy surface as she walked.

"Yes," he said, dropping the wagon handle and following her.

It took her forty paces to get around it, examining the mossy green sections and the gray and white lichen. When she got back to where she started, she looked up.

"Well, Mr. O'Connor, I wore my riding habit, so my skirt is not as constricting as my day gown, but I confess, I don't see the easiest path."

He stepped closer, pretending to study the rock as he placed a hand on either side of her.

"You might want to do that handy trick with your skirts the way you did when we climbed the tree."

He gazed down into her eyes, and Eleanor's stomach flipped delightfully, exactly as if jumping a fence on a good, swift horse.

"I shall do so, if you think it best."

He said nothing, staring down at her, his glance moving to her mouth.

She drew in a quick breath as his intentions were clear. He claimed her lips in a slow assault, and her knees weakened at once.

Thankfully, she had a rock, albeit a damp one, at her back, and the muscular planes of a man at her front. She opened her lips to him and let his tongue explore, unable to keep from sucking it gently.

When his hands left the rock and took hold of her waist, she sighed. Everything was perfect when he touched her and kissed her. She loved the smell of him, the feel of his cheeks, the way he tasted.

Her body was humming by the time he lifted his head.

"Kissing you is one of the most pleasurable things I have ever done."

One of them? Hm. Her thoughts flew to his trips to London, which Maggie had told her about. Kissing her, no matter how enjoyable, could not compete with making love to his paramours.

"Why did my remark make you look sad?"

She shook her head, refusing to disclose her jealousy. After all, at some point, if Grayson were being sincere and not toying with her affections, then she might experience the rest of the pleasures that occurred between a man and woman. The very same she'd seen animals do when she was younger—albeit she'd read it was more enjoyable than how it looked.

Moreover, she'd caught a glimpse of human mating during the Season when she'd inadvertently happened upon a couple in a garden during a ball, and once by wandering into the wrong room at a dinner party. They certainly seemed to be enjoying themselves.

"And now your smile is back," he said. "How I wish I could know your myriad and flittering thoughts."

She stroked his cheek with her gloved hand, already a little damp and leaving a dirty mark on his face. At the same time, somewhere far away to the east, there was an ominous roll of thunder.

"Show me the way up the rock, please."

"Yes, my lady." He returned to the wagon and slung the small sack over his head and shoulder, leaving his arms free while she reached between her legs and drew up her skirts to tuck into her waistband.

"Come around again," he instructed. "There are a few crevices in which to put your feet."

Sure enough, the second time around, when she wasn't solely looking upward at the boulder's height, she spied the fissures that cleaved it, top to bottom.

"I think it best if I stay below and give you a push from behind," Grayson said. "Should you fall back, I can catch you."

"Agreed," she said, despite having climbed many trees and even a few rocks in her life, as well as fence railings and stone walls, without ever falling.

With the toe of her boot in the lowest of the clefts and her hands finding purchase in the craggy rock sides, she drew herself up. While finding the next best place for her other foot, Eleanor shrieked and nearly let go as his hands took a firm hold of her bottom.

"Sorry to have startled you," he apologized. "Keep going. I'm right behind you."

"Yes, I had gathered that." Rolling her eyes, she continued upward.

The sarsen was about fifteen feet high and got narrower at the top, but after she reached the pinnacle, with Grayson occasionally putting a helpful hand on her rear end, she found a fairly level top of about eight yards in circumference, like a large stone table.

"Wonderful! The bishop's hostel. We have arrived."

Staying in the center, she peered over the side, then glanced out over the river. "The view!"

While still yards from the Great Ouse, there were no trees in front of them, and they had a private performance as it tumbled and raced along, frothing and churning.

Grayson stood beside her, feet planted, hands on his hips, admiring the view.

"It is rather wonderful, isn't it? Regardless, the farmers down river will feel happier when she settles back into her bed."

"She?" Eleanor mused.

He shrugged. "The way everyone refers to the river." Then he glanced down at her. "Shall we eat? I heard your stomach rumbling. I hope you brought bottles of—" he cut himself off. "Dammit all! I meant to tie the picnic basket to the rope and haul it up after."

She laughed at his forgetfulness. "How could you forget our picnic?" she teased. "We've talked about it for days."

"Truthfully?"

"Yes," she said.

"As soon as you started to climb and I touched your . . . touched you, every sensible thought went out of my brain."

She grinned. "Oh, so it's my fault?"

"Yes," he said emphatically, his arms going around her. "For being so enticing."

Enticing? Was she?

Grayson kissed her again, but Eleanor fought the usual delirium, mindful of being on a rather small area on a very high rock.

When he lifted his head, she asked him, "Have you ever brought anybody else up here?"

"Yes," he confessed immediately. "Cam, of course."

"Anyone else?"

"Are you a jealous wench?"

"Maybe I am," she said, thinking how novel and unwanted the feeling. But where Grayson was concerned, she had to confess, she felt proprietary.

"Only you," he promised. "Shall I go get the picnic basket?"

"Not until you show me the devil's seat. In any case, it wasn't my stomach rumbling, and you know it. But the thunder sounds quite far."

"Very well," he agreed. "We'll eat later. But we must get on our knees, for the seat is on the edge."

Doing as he said, Eleanor dropped to all fours and followed him to where the rock dropped away, not overlooking the river but cattycorner to it.

Before her was a vista of trees, which made sense when she considered Kidd's puzzle. They were looking, after all, for a large tree with at least seven branches.

And a death's head.

"This is the devil's seat," he said.

She stared, frowning. It wasn't more than a slight indentation in the rock's surface.

"Are you sure?"

"As sure as I am this is the bishop's hostel," he answered measuredly.

"But why would anyone call it such?"

"Sit upon it," he suggested.

She eased her legs over the side and fit her bottom into the indentation. It was obscenely uncomfortable, with a sharp rock digging in one soft cheek.

"Painful!" she exclaimed.

"And that's why. Only the devil himself would be happy seated there."

"Well, we're here now. Sit beside me, and let's use the spyglass."

CHAPTER FOURTEEN

Gray settled beside Eleanor, his legs dangling next to hers. He was peaceful, content, extremely happy, and irrevocably in love with this sweet miss.

Pulling the bag off his shoulder, he dug in it, pulled out the telescope, and handed it to her.

"Am I to do this?" she asked.

"You figured out most of the puzzle," he said. "You should spy the death's head first."

Her eyes sparkling up at him were nearly his undoing. He wanted to kiss her again, knew he always would, but at that moment, it was better to stick to the plan. Falling to their deaths in a lover's embrace was not the ending to this adventure he hoped for.

"Help me, then," Eleanor asked. "I haven't a clue."

He drew out the compass. Although figuring out degrees of latitude and longitude were not skills he truly possessed, since he'd hooked up the skull himself in the dark in the rainstorm, he could certainly fake the directions.

"First, we must find northeast by north, as the instructions said." He held out the compass as another rumble of thunder sounded, a little closer, causing the hair on the back of his neck to raise. The wind had shifted, too, heralding a rainstorm heading their way.

Holding the compass flat in front of him, he waited for the needle to settle and then showed her before pointing in the direction.

She lifted the spyglass to her eye and looked.

"Tell me if you see a tree with anything strange. When this was written, it was twenty-one degrees and thirteen minutes above the visible horizon."

"I have no idea what that means."

"In truth," he said, as thunder boomed again much closer, "I had to look it up." Glancing behind them, he saw the thunderheads rolling in from the horizon. They didn't have much time, and now, he feared, all they would get done was spotting the death's head and then have to seek cover.

"The horizon is zero and directly above us is ninety degrees, so twenty-one is about two of my fists up from the horizon."

Eleanor dutifully pointed the telescope in the direction and at the level in which he pointed. Unfortunately, it was growing darker quickly.

"What are minutes?" she asked.

"Trickier. Those are smaller than degrees, so I suggest you find the twenty-one degrees and then go up and down a little until you see—"

"Something white, like bones."

"Yes, exactly," he agreed. "If you see it, let me know."

"That's what I mean. I see something very white, like bleached bones. It is round and could be a skull."

"Remarkable!" He felt a thrill almost as if they were truly discovering Kidd's treasure.

"I'm focusing in on it," she said. "Yes! It is a skull, for I see eye sockets."

And then the first fat raindrops hit them.

"Bollocks," he said, not curbing his tongue around her, knowing she wouldn't mind.

"I suppose we'd best descend before we are skewered and sizzled by lightning," Eleanor said, not sounding the least frightened. "But first, mark which tree. Do you see it? Do you see the skull?"

She was still peering through the glass and pointing, waggling her finger around in front of her, which made him smile. If he didn't know which tree it was, he would not have been able to tell from her excited gesticulating.

"Yes, I see it now," he said. "It's an oak tree and has quite wide spacing between the branches. Good for climbing. If it were better weather, I would have you stay here while, with your direction, I went to mark it."

"That would be a good plan," she agreed. "But from the relation to the other trees and the river and the distance from this rock, I believe we can find the tree again from the ground."

"Time to go," he said.

Taking the telescope from her, he put it and the compass away. Shouldering the bag, he stood and offered her a hand. In a manner of minutes, they were on the ground once again, with their outer layers totally soaked.

"At least we're not in London," she reminded him, looking up with the brim of her tightly woven straw hat dripping.

He chuckled. "You are a gem, Eleanor. Come along. I know some shelter without having to go all the way back to the hall.

He and Cam had explored every inch of the riverbank between Turvey House and Angsley Hall. And this wasn't the first time he'd been caught in a storm. It was, however, the first he'd been caught with a beautiful woman. He hoped she would accept the humble shelter he knew was nearby.

An old fishing lean-to, which Lord Angsley kept in decent repair, greeted them a few yards along the river. He led her and the wagon into the small, three-sided structure made from planks, hoping she didn't mind the damp, musty smell of it. There were only tree stumps for seats, but the roof didn't leak, and he knew she would appreciate the unencumbered view.

"Perfect." She clapped her hands, looking around the cozy interior. "And now my stomach *is* rumbling. I do hope this rain shower passes over, and we can find the tree again." She settled onto one of the stumps.

"If we can't, we could leave the wagon with the shovel and other supplies here."

"A grand idea," Eleanor agreed, opening the basket and bringing out a stoppered bottle of lemonade and two beakers. She poured them each a cup and handed him one.

Next, she brought out four pickled eggs, which they ate ravenously.

"What else do you have in there?" He leaned over and tried to peek.

She laughed. "I have whatever I could grab quickly and be eaten with our hands. I have scones and thinly sliced ham, which you can roll and—"

He popped some ham in his mouth and took a bite of a scone. The rest was gone in a second bite. She handed him another scone and more ham, and then ate some herself, looking a darn sight daintier than he had.

"Delicious," he said. "Anything else?"

She laughed. "I hope we don't get stuck here for days because you have eaten all rations except the last. Yesterday's raspberry tarts from teatime." She handed him two, and he devoured them.

Watching her bite into a tart and seeing the sticky jam disappear into her mouth was dangerously arousing. He should have kept looking past the rain to the river rushing by. But it was too late. When she popped in the last bite and licked her lips, he groaned before he could stop himself.

Her eyes widened. She really had no idea how artlessly lovely she was or how she could inflame his desire with a smile or a flick of her pink tongue.

He had wanted her to find the treasure first before he went any further with their lovemaking. He had wanted her to know the depths of his feelings, as well as his intentions, which she would discover with the treasure. But the plans had gone awry, and the weather had contrived to put them alone in a shelter with a dry floor and no one nearby.

What's more, it was up to him to protect her virtue, to behave like a gentleman, and to restrain himself.

He grasped his fingers together in his lap and turned away from her.

ELEANOR HAD SEEN THE look in Grayson's eyes, and the answering call of her body frightened her. She yearned for him in every way, and knowing he felt it, too, and was experiencing the same intense desire made her do something extremely ill-advised.

Eleanor placed her hand on his thigh. His gaze flew to hers, and she nearly retreated. This was no timid boy she was playing with. This was a passionate, experienced man who was signaling one thing: *I want you.*

Moreover, he was struggling to rein in his passion. And she knew all the reasons for doing so. Their being alone even in this shelter, if discovered by certain people, maybe by anyone, would be her ruin. In London, she could never have headed out alone with him. Her reputation would be in tatters for climbing up a rock face with a man, never mind entering a lean-to and picnicking with him.

Why did the Angsleys tolerate such behavior?

Perhaps she and Grayson had hidden their attraction well. Or maybe things truly were less strict in the country. Or it could simply be the Angsleys looked upon Grayson as family, and she was the sister of John Angsley's wife.

What did that make her?

"I...," she trailed off.

What did she want to tell him?

"I am glad we finally got to start our adventure," she finished.

He seemed tense and frozen. With his jaw taut, Grayson reminded her of a cat in that moment before it pounced.

Eleanor swallowed, feeling a healthy measure of trepidation. No one knew where she was. It was thrilling! She was living the life of a Gothic heroine and loving every moment of it.

"You're smiling," he said. "A moment ago, you were not. Tell me what you are thinking."

She opened her mouth to speak when nearby thunder shook their lean-to. She shrieked with surprise, grabbing hold of him. Instantly, his arms went around her, drawing her onto his lap.

"It's all right," he soothed.

Her nerves remained on edge, especially now her breasts were crushed against his chest, and his hands were splayed across her back, feeling big and warm. Looking up, her eyes met his, their glances fusing.

His features twisted, beseeching and warning at the same time, as if tumultuous emotions were warring inside him.

"Grayson?" She had stripped off her gloves to eat. With bare fingers, she reached up and touched his face, stroking his cheek.

His eyes slammed closed, and she saw his throat bob with swallowing.

"Eleanor," he said, his voice thick and husky.

She still felt he was on the verge of snapping her up like a cat did its prey. Yet, she couldn't help herself. Entwining her fingers behind his neck, she sunk them into his hair. *Glorious!*

Then, she did the unthinkable. Using her grasp on his hair, she tugged him down to her, until their mouths were a whisper apart.

"Eleanor," he said again. It came out as a groan. "Have mercy," he added.

"Gray," she murmured against his lips, knowing she was behaving badly, but wanting more of him with every fiber of her being.

His eyes opened, and flames blazed in their depths as hot as any she'd ever stoked in the grate of a fireplace.

What happened next, she couldn't describe, for her world tilted suddenly. She assumed he would simply start to kiss her and closed her eyes in readiness. But then he lifted her from his lap. The next thing she knew, she was on her back, lying on her damp cloak on the dry ground.

From this vantage point, looking up at him, his face was in shadow, his expression unreadable. How she wished for a crackling fire beside them, not only because the rain had chilled her, but so she could see him better.

Lowering his head, he claimed her lips. This kiss felt entirely different than their previous ones because of their position. While he kept most of his weight on his forearms on either side of her, his legs were nestled between hers. If her skirts hadn't been tucked up for climbing, it wouldn't have been easily possible for him to settle, flanked by her thighs without raising her gown to her waist.

As the weight of his hips pressed into hers, she couldn't restrain from lifting her own to meet him. Her body sought to meld with his, seeking as close contact as possible.

After his skillful tongue had teased hers, he nibbled on her lower lip, and she sighed. His mouth left a trail of kisses along her jaw and down her slender neck, which she arched to give him better access. At the same time, she shivered, wanting more.

"My sweet," he murmured, opening the fastening at her throat so her cloak fell away entirely, giving him access to the skin at her collarbone.

When he tasted her with a gentle flick of his tongue, she moaned.

Her fingers clasped his shoulders, wishing she could touch more of him.

She could! There was no one there to stop her.

Trying to open his jacket while he was on top of her was a trial, especially while his hands roamed every part of her, and his mouth sought every inch of bare skin above her neckline.

She'd only succeeded in unfastening a few buttons when he rolled onto his back, taking her with him. She found herself splayed atop his body.

"I am a fiend," he declared, "and we must stop."

Still feeling a tingle where he'd kissed her neck and her décolletage, her body humming with pleasure, Eleanor didn't want to stop and told him so, but he held her hands still on his chest.

"Remove your jacket," she ordered him, "and your shirt so I can touch you."

Grayson actually laughed at her. *Mortifying!*

"Why are you laughing?" She sat up, looking down at him, feeling tendrils of her hair falling around her face.

Oh, dear. She would have to fix that before she saw anyone.

Then she caught her breath, for he looked divinely handsome, lying beneath her, wearing a rueful grin.

"Because you look more like a woodland fairy than ever, despite wearing a petulant expression. And because I cannot undress here, and you know it. We must tidy up and behave like civilized people."

Still seated astride his hips, she could feel the heat of him coursing up through the layers of fabric that separated them, permeating the soft place between her legs. Yanking her hands free, she crossed her arms over her still tingling nipples.

"Civilized people!" she scoffed. "Those refined ninnies in the ballrooms do this kind of thing in the back gardens of every venue during the Season. I stumbled upon more than one tryst while escaping the stuffy rooms and simply trying to get a little air."

He laughed again. "I'm sure that made you extremely unpopular. Imagine how we'd feel if a snoopy Miss So-and-So barged in upon us at this moment."

"Snoopy! I never barge," she declared. "And we are doing far less than what I saw others doing, believe me. Sometimes girls were lying back on a bench or even bent forward over a stone wall with their skirts over their heads, and the men were—"

"I get the idea," he said, sounding displeased. "You were probably outside too much for your chaperone's liking."

"At least I was alone," she said, then felt her cheeks heat up. She sounded like a prudish innocent.

"Mostly alone," she added, hoping she sounded more worldly.

As if he hadn't heard her, he said, "I respect you too much to continue down the path we're on, no matter how pleasurable."

With Grayson struggling to get up while she sat on him, Eleanor had no choice but to climb off or be dumped unceremoniously onto the ground. It was impossible not to be annoyed as all the wonderful sensations ceased, and she was left with only longing and frustration.

He took her hand as they rose to their feet.

"We are a sorry sight," he said.

She didn't care. He had rejected her, and easily, it seemed. For him, it had been *merely* pleasurable. For her, it had felt earthshattering, and she'd been prepared to give him all of her.

Now, he was worried about appearances, and she wanted to scream.

Withdrawing her hand from his, she decided she could be as calm as he was, and she set about to smoothing her skirts. First, she pulled them from the waistband and let them fall around her feet again. Then she reached behind her and shook her cloak, all without looking at him.

He respected her, did he? She would rather he'd been so overcome with desire . . . and love . . . he couldn't help himself from making her his woman in that most intimate way.

"Your hair," he began, but she stopped him with a look.

"I will tuck it up under my hat. Where is my hat?"

They both spied where it had fallen, and retrieving it before she could, he held it out to her. She snatched it without a word of thanks, which wasn't like her.

"And then I will put my cloak hood over the entire mess," she added testily, "until I get back safely in my room."

He still stared at her, absently wiping his large hands down his pants and over his jacket to remove any stray clumps of dirt.

"I hope you realize why we had to stop. I fear you are too young to understand what nearly occurred."

She had been looking out into the pouring rain when he spoke those loathsome words. She whirled around to face him.

"That is the stupidest thing you have ever said to me, Mr. O'Connor. I am leaving."

With that, she fastened her cloak at her neck, raised the hood over her hat, and walked out into the storm.

Let him deal with the picnic basket, and let the devil take him!

CHAPTER FIFTEEN

Gray watched Eleanor stride ahead of him, radiating fury, and he didn't attempt to catch up. He had inadvertently offended her. Some part of him still wanted to protect her from . . . himself.

He knew she was a woman—*God, did he know!*—but the part of him that recalled the innocent girl from five years earlier definitely didn't want her first time to be on the dirty floor of a fishing lean-to.

He was absolutely certain, nonetheless, he wanted her first time to be with him. And every time after that. For the rest of their lives.

Clearly, she didn't care he was the son of a servant. They treated each other as equals, and a marriage between them would be a satisfying union. But he didn't want to blurt out his intention after having gone to so much trouble to set up the game.

Wondering how to make amends, he kept her in his sights on the long walk back, yet not really fearing she could get into trouble marching hell-bent toward Angsley Hall.

She entered through the terrace door, disappearing from his view, and he followed a few moments later. It was a sad ending to their otherwise enjoyable escapade.

Glancing at her Wellies, which looked as if they'd been hurled toward the mudroom, he removed his own before tucking all of them tidily out of the way, and then hanging up his sodden jacket.

Some dry clothing and hot tea were in order. Maybe he could even coax her to have the latter with him. Heading along the passageway to the main stairs, Gray was halted by the ever-present Mr. Stanley.

"Mr. O'Connor, a missive from the Earl of Cambrey arrived while you were out."

Gray hoped nothing had befallen Maggie. Taking the note off the silver tray, he read it.

Dammit! He was needed back at once. He supposed it was about time he took back the mantle of being an estate manager. Two of the workhorses were displaying symptoms of colic, and their stablemaster wanted to consult with him. A blight in one section of the orchard was confounding the head gardener, who had some ideas to run past him. A strange crack had appeared in the drawing room ceiling, and the butler believed Mr. O'Connor would know of the best plasterer in the area. As a matter of fact, he did.

It was time to get home. They could leave after lunch if one of the Angsley maids could get Eleanor's trunks packed. At least in the privacy of the carriage on the short trip to Turvey House, he could try to soothe her insulted womanhood.

When she didn't come downstairs in a timely fashion, and he'd cooled his heels drinking a pot of tea and idly chatting with whichever Angsley happened by, he sent a maid up to tell Eleanor she must pack. Then Gray headed back outside. The rain had stopped entirely, as the breeze had blown the thick, dark clouds far to the west. He would tell his mother of his imminent departure and assure her he would see her as soon as possible.

To his surprise, her door was locked again. He rapped at the cheerfully painted door, recalling when Lady Angsley declared each should be done in a rich blue to let the retired servants know they were cared about. Her ladyship had told him and Cam about it at dinner a couple years earlier, seemingly oblivious to the fact that one of those servants was his mother.

There, but for the grace of God, a thorough education, and having made a goodly amount in the stock market, went he. The blue door would *never* be his lot in life.

He jiggled the handle again. There was a brief delay as before, and then to his surprise, Eleanor answered.

"I don't know how that got locked," she muttered, looking at his feet and not his face. "I suppose I must have inadvertently done it."

Then she stood back so he could see his mother seated at the table, the same lacework laid before her. To his eyes, they had made little progress, but then he knew nothing of the intricacy of such work.

"I had no idea you'd left the main house," he said to Eleanor before greeting his mother.

"Tea, dear?" she asked him.

"No, thank you. I just had some. I was waiting for you to come down," he said, turning to Eleanor, unable to keep the irritation from his voice.

She shrugged, looking sullen.

When he considered the passionate creature who had been lying beneath him an hour earlier—the one who had wanted to undress him!—he wished he could magically bring her back. Doubtless, he could do so when he had a private moment to explain himself.

But not in front of his mother, who was watching them carefully.

"I came to tell you we have to leave."

Eleanor's glance flew to meet his, her face already looking mutinous.

"I thought we agreed with Maggie not truly being ill, there was no rush."

"No rush for you," he said, "but I have work to do. They need me back on the estate. Things are starting to go awry."

"Then you may go," Eleanor said, sounding positively like a royal highness dismissing her knight.

"You must come with me," he said.

"Why must I?"

Her hands on her hips was not a good sign. Moreover, he realized his mother's head was going back and forth as if watching lawn tennis.

"Because Turvey House was your destination," he pointed out.

She hesitated, shooting his mother a glance.

"I am not ready to leave."

Eleanor was simply being obstinate. There was nothing to keep her here . . . except Kidd's treasure.

"We can come back within days to finish our adventure," he said. His mother would think they were barmy, but what could he do?

With a wave of her hand, Eleanor dismissed his words. "It's not that."

Really? "Then what?"

She levelled him with a glare. "I do not answer to you, Mr. O'Connor."

At this, his mother's eyes widened, and she turned away, obviously not wanting to be witness to their tiff.

"True, you don't," he agreed. "But the easiest way and the best time for you to finish your journey to Turvey House is with me today."

"Today? That's impossible. Even if I agreed, I couldn't get all my things packed before dark."

"That's why I waited for you downstairs to tell you to gather your things."

"But I was here," Eleanor pointed out, as if she were being reasonable.

"I didn't know that." He realized he was speaking through clenched teeth and tried to relax his jaw. "Why don't you want to leave?" This time, he tried to keep his tone light.

"I cannot say."

For pity's sake. She was trying his patience. "Cannot or will not?"

"Both." She resumed her seat at his mother's table.

"Is it the lacework?"

"Perhaps, among other things. I am not trying to be difficult." Eleanor glanced at his mother. "I will come along soon. When do you leave?"

He hesitated. Truly, he had no control over Eleanor, and he had to accept that. However, it rankled him all the same.

"In an hour at the most." He ran a hand through his hair, feeling ill at ease leaving her behind, then he recalled another compelling reason for her to go with him.

"But your birthday," he protested. "You'll be here alone."

"Your birthday?" his mother exclaimed, turning to Maggie.

"In a few days," she admitted, keeping her gaze on him. "Anyway, won't you come back?" For the first time, she sounded uncertain.

"Yes, when I can," he promised. "But I wouldn't have to leave my work and return here so quickly if you would come with me now. Besides, you should be with Maggie and Cam at Turvey."

"I will see them soon enough."

"Very well." He was getting nowhere. Leaning down, he kissed his mother on the cheek. "Keep an eye on her."

His mother nodded. "Of course."

"I don't need anyone to—" Eleanor began, but he cut her off.

"I know what you're going to say. You don't need an eye on you." He shook his head.

Desperately, Gray wanted to kiss her and make things right, but he couldn't do it here. "Will you come say goodbye."

"I...," Eleanor faltered, her cheeks immediately reddening, and she glanced at his mother. He would have laughed at her obvious display of emotion if she weren't annoying him to Kingdom come.

In any case, she stood and followed him out the door.

WHAT COULD ELEANOR TELL him? She couldn't abandon Mrs. O'Connor, not when the woman had broken down in tears over her secret. Besides, it truly wouldn't take long to teach her to write. Grayson's mother was clever and quick.

"I want you to come with me," he repeated when they were out of his mother's hearing.

"We just went over this," she reminded him. "Did you invite me out here to say goodbye properly or to argue further?"

"You are being childish," he persisted.

Eleanor hadn't expected that remark. She'd hoped he had moved past his initial impression of her as too young for a relationship. She'd shown herself to be smart enough to figure out the puzzle, and if he only knew, she was being dependable and keeping her word to his mother.

"First, you called me selfish. I don't think I am, and I didn't appreciate it. And now childish. I don't believe I am that, either. Still, I don't have to explain myself to you."

"I called you selfish because I was worried you would go to Turvey House and get sick, and I couldn't bear it. I'm calling you childish because I fear you will get into mischief if left to your own devices here at Angsley Hall. Without me."

He truly didn't see her as a responsible adult.

"Without a nanny, you mean?"

"No. I didn't mean that at all. But I don't want you climbing trees and searching for something that isn't there." He ran a hand through his hair and looked decidedly distraught.

"All signs point to us being on the right path. How do you know it isn't there?"

"Because I made it all up," he said softly.

He might as well have shouted the words, for they hit her like a punch to her stomach. They also addled her brain.

Hadn't he found the mysterious piece of paper in a book?

"I don't understand," she said, her voice barely above a whisper.

For a moment, he said nothing. Then he shook his head. "I made up the idea that William Kidd was ever here in Bedfordshire."

How terrible of him! She had never taken Grayson for a liar.

"You tricked me? On purpose?" *Had he wanted to make a fool of her?*

It took a moment for his gaze to meet hers. Then he answered, "Yes."

"I don't believe you," she snapped back. He was obviously saying this to stop her from going any farther without him. "How can you explain the rock and the devil's seat, and even the skull? You couldn't have made up a giant boulder."

"Only the names." Then he let out a long sigh. "Actually, the names exist, but I applied them to our local places."

"You are still not making sense. Exist where?"

"In a story," he confessed. "A Gothic tale by Poe."

"No!" she protested. "You're only saying this so I won't search without you. I've climbed many trees, Mr. O'Connor, and had many adventures. I don't intend to stop when you are not by my side. But you don't have to destroy this wonderful quest by lying about it."

"You're being unreasonable. I'm telling you the truth. I only did it to please you."

Eleanor had never felt so betrayed or foolish.

"And now you're being cruel. I have a task to do here completely unrelated to your silly, fantastical game, and you shall not dissuade me from finishing it. I made a promise to someone, and I will keep it."

His eyes narrowed. "To whom?"

She kept her lips firmly pressed together.

"Is it dangerous?" he demanded.

She threw her hands up in the air. "Of course not!"

"I shall return for you as soon as I can. Maybe even for your birthday."

"I can climb into the Angsleys' carriage any time and come by myself. I travelled all the way from Sheffield, for goodness' sake! I can handle two miles to Turvey!"

She realized she was practically yelling. Taking a deep, steadying breath, she added more calmly, "And I shall write my sister a note explaining everything."

"Everything?" he snapped at once. "You mean you'll tell her whatever it is you're not telling me?"

Again, she clamped her lips closed. *What an infuriating man!*

"Very well." He turned on his heel, but he only got a few steps before he turned back to her. "I didn't intend to hurt or trick you. I only wanted to amuse you with the hunt for pirate treasure."

She lifted her chin. "As if I'm a child to be entertained. And what you said in the shelter? You think I am too young to know my own mind and feelings, or to understand the world. You're wrong!"

He nodded. "I only meant . . . I'm not going to explain myself right here and now. Just don't be angry with me, Eleanor. It's too hard to leave without seeing your lovely smile."

She looked away from him. He was dear to her, and she ardently wished he wasn't leaving, despite being furious with him.

"Please," he beseeched.

She gave him the best smile she could.

"A watery version of your usual one, but I'll take it."

Even though they were standing in front of his mother's window, and anyone could be watching from the main house or the stables or anywhere, he leaned close and set a kiss upon her lips.

It was over before she realized Grayson's intent. Then she watched him walk away, broad shoulders rigid and straight.

Blast! Dashing away the sudden tears that welled in her eyes and spilled onto her cheeks, she reminded herself she was not a child. Everything would not always go her way. She was a woman with a task to attend to, and he was a man with employment.

Squaring her shoulders as he had done, she returned to Mrs. O'Connor, knowing she was going to have to spend time reassuring Grayson's mother all was well, despite not being entirely sure of that herself.

He had lied to her for days!

CHAPTER SIXTEEN

Eleanor sat in her room before dinner, all the amusement gone from Angsley Hall with the departure of Grayson. She and Mrs. O'Connor had worked well into the afternoon. His mother was motivated and determined. Eleanor was confident she would not only be writing, but be able to read, as well.

To that end, she'd ventured into the nursery to discover what children's primers might be there. Nanny Wendall let her come away with a chapbook of both capital and lowercase letters, phonics lessons, and phrases. It had a bright green cover and woodcuts of a cock and a horse. Eleanor hoped its simplicity would not offend Mrs. O'Connor.

She also found an older book, *Cobwebs to Catch Flies*, by the so-called Mrs. Lovechild. She supposed it didn't matter that it was from the last century. After all, reading and writing hadn't changed much. Moreover, these books would be easier for Grayson's mother to practice with than the books from Lord Angsley's library.

Meanwhile, Eleanor tried to pen letters to Beryl and Maggie and even to her mother and Jenny. Her mind kept drifting to her last conversation with Grayson. He professed to have taken something from a Poe story and somehow melded it with their world here in Bedfordshire. At the moment, she had to believe him, although she could only wonder at the extent to which he had gone.

Had he made up the code and the message and even climbed a tree and nailed a skull to it?

Having fruitlessly searched the library for any works by Edgar Allan Poe, she could only determine Grayson had removed any or had known the story by heart. She would find out eventually when she continued on to Turvey House and had a chance to speak with him.

Her letters half written, she went down to dinner, and afterward, sat by a low fire, drinking port and letting Lady Angsley tell her all the news. Not only did her ladyship enjoy a local paper, she also had papers delivered from Town, just as Eleanor's own mother did.

While sometimes the London news was a little stale, it normally held her interest. Occasionally, one of her sisters' husbands was mentioned, and that always delighted her. Tonight, Eleanor tried to pay attention, but her mind kept wandering to the wonderful time high upon the bishop's hostel and their intimate moment in the shelter by the river. Then, she replayed his surprising confession of duplicity.

It saddened her to think he had lied to her, even if he'd done it with the best of intentions to entertain her. While she'd worked hard to decipher the pirate's code, Grayson had already known the answer. It irked her to have been made a fool.

And to think how terrible she'd felt even lightly hedging about what she was doing with his mother. Lying was a terrible sin, she'd always believed. If her father had been truthful, her mother would have been prepared for the confusion following his death, the money-grubbing debt collectors, the maelstrom of selling off their townhouse and belongings, and their flight home to their country cottage in Sheffield.

Thank God for the cottage, or she and her sisters, her mother, and even the few servants they'd kept would all have been homeless.

Obviously, Grayson's prevarication was not on the same caliber of seriousness. But she didn't like to think she hadn't been able to tell the truth from his lies.

After a few hands of *écarte* with Lady Angsley, unable to focus and losing each time, Eleanor bid her hostess good night.

Tomorrow, she would approach Mrs. O'Connor first thing, knowing she was an early-to-bed, early-to-rise person. They could get as much learning in as Grayson's mother could handle.

Climbing under her covers, not in the mood for any of the Gothic romances piled beside her bed, Eleanor picked up Mrs. Lovechild's *Cobwebs to Catch Flies*. The introduction began with "To my little readers: Do not imagine that, like a great spider, I will give you a hard gripe and infuse venom to blow you up."

Eleanor laughed out loud. *Gracious!* That seemed a little scary for being a children's primer, but it worked to lure her to read more. Thumbing through it, she enjoyed the writer's cheeky and, at the same time, cheerful tone in the stories, combined with a little menace to keep the children alert and interested. It seemed there was a hint of danger at the fair, and a naughty boy who didn't listen to his father on the way to school.

Indeed, there was a touch of Gothic everywhere. When she drifted off to sleep, she had a terrible nightmare about spiders.

AS EXPECTED, MRS. O'CONNOR was a natural. Eleanor believed it was the woman's attention to tiny stitches during her whole life, but she never wrote an *o* when an *a* was needed, and she did not mix up her *u*'s with her *v*'s. Her script looked almost as if she'd been writing for years.

Seated beside Grayson's mother while she practiced and asked questions, Eleanor finished her letters to her family and her brief note to Maggie. And then she thought better of sending it. It would be more fun to surprise her sister in a day.

She'd had a little surprise of her own that morning. Mrs. O'Connor had not been at home upon Eleanor's early arrival. Deciding to wait, she'd stood happily drinking in the sights, sounds, and fresh smells of the morning, leaning a little lazily against the granary wall.

Suddenly, she'd seen Grayson's mother appear as if approaching from the main house, on the very path Eleanor had just traversed.

How strange! Even stranger when Mrs. O'Connor startled at seeing Eleanor and had a decidedly flustered air. They entered the suite of rooms, which were cool and closed up.

Plainly, Mrs. O'Connor had not vacated her home earlier that morning for a quick visit with Cook at Angsley Hall. Eleanor would wager her Wellies Grayson's mother hadn't slept there the night before.

While it was absolutely none of her business, Eleanor's next thought was of Mr. Stanley. And she took another look at Mrs. O'Connor. She was not old, after all, nor was the butler. In fact, they were both fit and healthy, and of approximately the same age, as near as Eleanor could tell.

Regardless, she couldn't think of them behaving in the manner she and Grayson had in the library, or in the lean-to—*definitely not!* But Eleanor could imagine them enjoying a warm and happy companionship.

And, why not?

Hoping to ease any embarrassment Mrs. O'Connor was feeling, Eleanor had remarked on what a wonderful morning it was for a brisk walk and said yes to a cup of tea. Then, they had plunged into their lessons, the first of three sets they would have that day.

By mid-morning, two days later, Mrs. O'Connor looked at Eleanor with tears in her eyes.

"I believe I have learned all I need in order to write to my son."

Eleanor nodded. "It is inspiring how quickly you have picked this up. I'm sure you can have more paper from the writing desk when this runs out. And Mrs. Wendall said you can return the primers to the nursery at your leisure."

With a hug and a promise to see her again soon, Eleanor asked her maid to begin packing.

Feeling extremely grown up, she refrained from returning to the bishop's hostel and did not attempt to climb the tree where she had plainly seen some type of skull high up overhead.

If it was all a farce, then what was the point?

After the short carriage ride, Eleanor arrived to emotional hugs and kisses from Maggie, who glowed, not because she was with child, but because she always radiated a dewy beauty, which was the envy of every woman in London.

Her husband was a handsome, charming man. Eleanor suspected he'd been a bit of a rake before Maggie won him over and tamed him. The earl caught Eleanor up in a hug and twirled her around.

"I'm going to be a father!" John said to her.

"You already are," she reminded him with a laugh as he set her down.

"Twice blessed," he said. "And each time will be just as big a blessing. Turvey House has room for twenty children."

"Twenty?" Maggie shrieked before they all laughed.

"Where is Grayson?" Eleanor asked, as it seemed odd he wasn't there to greet her as well.

When two pairs of eyes widened, she amended, "I mean, Mr. O'Connor, but we are now on a friendly footing and using our given names. Not to shock you," she finished.

"No," John said, his expression a little smug. "It doesn't shock me."

"Everything surprises me," Maggie admitted. "Let's have coffee and a good chin-wag. You can tell me all about your friendly footing and how everyone is faring at Angsley Hall. That young Miss Phoebe is going to be the belle of the ball one day soon."

It was over coffee Eleanor learned Grayson was not at Turvey House at all.

"He put everything to rights here, as he always does," John said. "I don't know what we would do without him."

Maggie smiled at her husband. "I suppose you would have to get your hands dirty now and again, my lord."

"Are you saying I am lazy?" John put an arm around his wife's shoulders and drew her closer to him on the sofa.

Maggie laughed again. Eleanor had a feeling they spent a great deal of time playfully teasing one another.

"In any case," John continued, "after Gray finished, he hightailed it to London as he does every so often."

Eleanor's dismay was instantaneous, having been certain he would be at Turvey House and having prepared herself to see him again. Her thwarted anticipation, mostly pleasant with a sliver of anxiousness, left her entirely deflated.

"Hadn't he only just returned from London before I arrived at Angsley Hall?"

"True," Maggie said. "I was confined to my room and didn't even get to see him before he went there to tell you not to come." She glanced at the earl and added, "Because of my ridiculously over-protective husband!"

"Did you send him back to London on Turvey House matters?" Eleanor asked her brother-in-law.

"No. Late yesterday, Gray said he needed to go to London, and while he is my estate manager, he is not my servant. If he wants to go to Town or to Paris, for that matter, I cannot stop him."

Grayson went away for personal reasons.

Maggie had previously told her he went there for *entertainment*, but she doubted he'd gone all that way to see a play or an opera. Her instinct told her one thing—Grayson had gone away because of one of his lady-friends.

Perhaps his passions had been so inflamed and then so frustrated by their last encounter, he needed to slake them. She'd read how it worked for men. It was not uncommon for their desires to need release, hence the vast numbers of ladies of the night.

"Did he say when he is returning?" she asked.

"Are you well?" Maggie asked her. "You look peaked."

"I'm fine. Perhaps tired from the journey."

Her sister laughed. "It was only a couple of miles."

"True," Eleanor agreed, "but I stayed up late reading. Do you mind if I go and unpack?"

"Of course not. I'm simply thrilled you made it for your birthday. I have a sweet treat planned, and Mummy and Jenny both sent cards, which I shall give you tomorrow."

"How thoughtful," Eleanor said, but she was disappointed, nonetheless. She wanted to see Grayson, and now, he wouldn't even be there for her birthday.

THE DAY DAWNED CLEAR, which meant nothing as clouds could blow up on a moment's notice, and it might be raining by midday. However, it allowed Eleanor to take her morning walk before breakfast. The grounds of Turvey House were one of her favorite walking places. They had orchards and gardens, paddocks and fields of wildflowers. You could hear the river, still swollen from all the recent storms, rushing and tumbling nearby.

And there was Grayson's lovely house, larger than a cottage, more polished than a farmhouse, it was a modest brick residence of two stories with plenty of windows. She'd only been inside it once with Maggie and Beryl, when the three of them strolled over there a year earlier to take the estate manager some freshly baked goods in trade for his help fastening a long swing to one of the oaks.

Inside, there were polished wooden floors, painted wainscoting, and thick Persian carpets, stone hearths, and large casual furniture, designed for comfort more than for style. It was the perfect blend of elegance and coziness. She'd particularly liked the herbs drying upside-down from his pantry ceiling, knowing he had placed them there himself since he had no cook.

Her favorite part of his house, however, was not inside it but on top. A captain's walk, Grayson called the large railed platform atop his roof, or a widow's watch, depending on who was asked or who was upon it. Instead of looking over an ocean, however, the rooftop platform offered a view of the horizon in every direction and the River Great Ouse weaving across the lush green landscape like a silvery ribbon.

At night, he said he often took a telescope, far larger than the spyglass they'd used at Angsley House, up to the captain's walk. With it, he would sit for hours looking at the stars. Eleanor had done the same thing many times from her family's Sheffield cottage back garden, without the benefit of a spyglass.

Glancing up at the platform, Eleanor wished he was there, waiting for her to climb the small circular stairs from the second floor to the roof. How she would love to stand beside him and look at the view.

But he had gone to London.

Circling past his home, she walked onward to the river's edge. There were no woods here, just grass to the riverbank. It was easier to fish than from the Angsley estate.

She smiled, recalling how Grayson considered her quite the competent fisherwoman the last time she had cast her pole with him, mostly because she could bait her hook by herself without being squeamish.

Eleanor sighed to herself. She fared so much better in the country than in London, and all along, she believed

Grayson admired her because of it. Yet her inclination to the natural world apparently made her seem childish. And she couldn't shake the ominous feeling she had driven him away with her ridiculous Wellies and her lack of polish.

If he didn't have estate business to do in London, then it could only be the temptations of more sophisticated, worldly women which had drawn him away from her.

And on her birthday, too.

Hearing Maggie calling her name from the back terrace, Eleanor set her steps in the direction of the manor, trying to tamp down the irrational hope Grayson had returned.

CHAPTER SEVENTEEN

Maggie and John made it a perfect birthday. They laughed all day long over the silliest things. The earl took Eleanor riding, not allowing Maggie "in her condition" to go. Afterward, they practiced archery and then played lawn bowls. Eleanor was positive she would beat the earl, and they were momentarily tied, but then, against all odds, Maggie won.

"Imagine that," Maggie said, not usually the sporty type.

The river was running too fast for fishing, so they spent the rest of the daylight playing one-on-one croquet.

They had dinner and birthday cake before the clouds rolled in. Strangely, even though Eleanor could smell rain in the air, none was yet falling at Turvey House.

"Like a birthday miracle," John vowed. "I am beyond tired of this weather. Is it too much to ask for a stretch of sunshine?"

"At least we're not in London," Eleanor said, recalling her conversation with Grayson. "Only think how disgusting the streets are during and after a storm."

"True. That reminds me. I have something Gray left for you," her brother-in-law said quite casually.

Eleanor sat up straighter on the sofa. She'd already had her mother's and sisters' cards, as well as a cameo broach from Maggie and a new sidesaddle from her brother-in-law.

"Really?"

"Well, he didn't tell me to give it to you, but he left it in the library and said he had planned to give it to you for your birthday," John clarified. "Actually, he said something about giving it to you sooner if things hadn't gone awry. Honestly, the man left so fast, he was talking nonsense."

"Will you give it to me now, please?" Eleanor asked, excitement building. Grayson hadn't simply gone away and forgotten her.

John disappeared and came back a minute later. "It's not even properly wrapped for a present, and I don't think it's new anyway."

He handed her a small brown-paper parcel. She could tell by the feel of it exactly what it was—a book.

Tearing off the wrapper, she shrieked in delight and held it to her chest, beaming at Maggie and John.

"Whatever is it?" Maggie asked.

"*The Gold Bug!*" Eleanor declared.

"A bug?" her sister demanded.

"Edgar Allan Poe's story, a collection of them actually, which includes *The Gold Bug*. Grayson and I had a bit of a lark pretending to follow the same adventure as in the story." Eleanor stopped at the looks on their faces. In any case, she didn't want to explain everything; she simply must begin reading immediately.

Standing up, she went to her sister on the opposite sofa and kissed her cheek. "Good night. Thank you for a wonderful birthday, the cake, the dinner, everything."

"The expensive saddle and jewelry," the earl added with a sideways grin.

"Oh, yes!" Eleanor returned to snatch up her broach and her greeting cards. The saddle was on the chair.

Glancing at it uncertainly, not wanting to delay reading her book, she asked, "Shall I take it to the stables?"

"No," John said. "It's nearly dark. We'll take care of it in the morning and go for another ride."

"Are you really going off to bed to read this early?" Maggie asked.

"If you don't mind,'" Eleanor entreated, holding the book out in explanation.

"It's your birthday," Maggie said. "You may spend it how you like."

HALF AN HOUR LATER, Eleanor knew exactly how she would like to spend the remainder of her birthday. She also knew her sister and John would not like it one bit. It was only eight o'clock, however, and early by any civilized notion. Why, she could still consider it practically daytime, late afternoon even.

A perfect time for a ride.

Wearing her dark green habit and creeping down the stairs, she was thrilled to see the drawing room empty. Snatching up her new saddle, she slipped out the front door, knowing she was less likely to encounter a nosey servant, or even John and Maggie, who often sat out on the back terrace.

Keeping to the shadows as best she could, she made her way to the stables, knowing exactly which stall held the gentle mount Grayson normally gave her to ride.

"Bess," Eleanor whispered to the horse, not wanting to startle her. She was dozing at this hour. Opening the stall gate, as she entered, the mare whinnied softly.

"Shall we have a little adventure, my girl?"

First placing a blanket over the horse's back, she then hoisted the saddle over, before cinching and buckling it. She'd been tacking up horses since she was old enough to ride, and used to stand on a step to do so. Grabbing a harness from a peg, she slipped the bit into Bess's willing mouth and then fastened it over the horse's head and behind her ears.

"Good girl." As she began leading the horse out of the stables, she heard the scuffle of footsteps.

"What are you doing?" The voice behind her making her jump could only belong to the stable boy, the lowest one in the pecking order, who slept in the straw most nights.

Having prepared herself for possibly being intercepted, Eleanor had managed not to shriek as if guilty.

"Good day. You are Jaime, aren't you?"

"Yes, miss." In the waning light, she could see his eyes darting around, and she feared he would run off to get someone in authority before she could convince him to let her go.

"How are you this fine . . . late afternoon?"

"Well, miss. Where are you taking Bess?"

"Why, for a ride of course. Beautiful evening, don't you think? Sun is still . . . on the horizon. I'd better hurry before I lose the light completely."

"No one said anyone would be taking a horse out tonight," he protested.

"You know me. I love to ride. It's my birthday today."

"Happy birthday, miss."

"Thank you. I was given a new saddle, and I simply intend to ride around the estate once or twice to try it out."

"Does his lordship know, miss?"

"He was the one who gave me the saddle, Jaime."

The lad hesitated, and Eleanor was extremely relieved at not lying about the earl having given her permission. If Jaime took it that way, however, she would be very pleased.

"Very well, miss," he said at last. "I'll be here to help you when you get back. Soon," he added, hopefully.

"Thank you. And since you're here, would you like to give me a leg up?"

With a nod, he cupped his hands and helped her draw up easily into the saddle. She hooked her leg over the pommel.

ELEANOR

"Perfect," she said, smiling down at him. "Again, thank you. I'll see you soon."

Soon was such a nebulous word, she assured herself as she set off directly toward Angsley Hall.

BESS WAS CANTERING SMOOTHLY, and the moon seemed to be keeping its glowing face out from behind the clouds, although Eleanor could see they were thickening to the east, behind her.

It only took her fifteen minutes to traverse the two miles and get to the lean-to and their abandoned supplies. That gave her plenty of time to muse upon Poe's delightful story. Not a Gothic, terrifying tale like Shelley's *Frankenstein*, it had been more an intellectual exercise with the very strange and seemingly inexplicable peppered in.

When she'd read the ending with the protagonist finding the buried pirate treasure, Eleanor knew Grayson would have buried something for her to find.

Dismounting, she found everything as they'd left it at the fishing shelter, but she couldn't ride Bess and pull the wagon. Tethering the horse to a branch, Eleanor lit the oil lamp, enjoying its cheerful glow. Without wasting any time, she began dragging the small cart toward the oak twenty feet past the bishop's hostel.

It was easy to find. From the base of the tree, she could look back and see the devil's seat high upon the boulder. Above her, she could even see the white skull catching the moonlight. While she very much doubted it was a human death head, since Grayson was not a fierce pirate, she would soon find out.

Tucking up her skirts, Eleanor took the string with the small kitchen weight already threaded onto it from the supplies. There was nothing else she needed up in the tree.

The lantern would have to stay in the wagon for she couldn't climb and hold onto it.

Then, as she and Grayson had been going to do together, she began to climb the oak.

With a wry smile, she realized he'd chosen a tree which, while following the dictates of *The Gold Bug*, was also an easy climb. The thick branches were close together so she could easily reach the first one and each subsequent one.

As she made her way up the tree, her only wish was for more light. With each passing minute, it grew darker, and, unfortunately, the creepy crawlies of the night had come out. As she placed her hand on the next branch, a spider crawled across her glove, and she screamed before she could stop herself.

Then Eleanor laughed, breaking the tension that had built in her. She was not afraid of spiders, nor snakes. It was simply the shock of the first encounter. There were bound to be more, but she truly hoped none were dropping onto her pinned hat.

In another ten minutes, having encountered nothing more frightening than a few bats and more spiders whom she startled in their webs, she reached the branch with the skull. Grayson must have come out on the night she saw the wet footprints in the hallway and set up the clue. *How sweet of him!*

Just as the servant Jupiter had done in the short story, Eleanor worked her way out onto the end of the branch. It turned out to be a goat skull, very old, the bone already bleached white, and held in place with a big nail.

She shivered. After all, it was not every night a girl found herself high in a tree with a skull of the once living. And on her twentieth birthday, too!

If Grayson could see her now, he would be appalled. Again, she laughed.

Crack! The first bolt of lightning split the dark sky, miles away over the river. The heated air boomed a moment later.

Oh, dear! She had best hurry.

"What's next?" she asked herself aloud, recalling very well what she had to do. Untying the string from around her neck, she held it directly over the left eye socket. According to the story, and to the puzzle she'd deciphered, she had to let it fall through the skull. The small iron weight from Cook's kitchen scale would ensure it went down straight to mark a spot directly below.

Another sizzling lightning bolt lit up the night, which she appreciated, as she let the weight fall from her fingers, watching it take the string to the ground and fall into the grass.

Boom! The thunder, closer now, seemed to shake the oak tree, and even caused the bats to fly about for a moment before they settled down again. Eleanor clapped her hands with excitement. She must move more quickly, or it would be pitch black and she would never finish the quest.

Climbing down was always a little harder and slower than up. Still, she was nimble, moving as fast as she could, and not minding when her dress caught more than once. Each time, she yanked, and eventually, it tore. She didn't care. After all, Mrs. O'Connor was an excellent seamstress.

Nearly giddy with the excitement of her success so far, she jumped the last few feet to the ground, and her riding boot slipped on the damp grass.

The devil!

Gasping as her ankle twisted sharply, she held her foot up in the air for a painful moment. She should have worn her Wellies!

Could she walk? Testing her footing, applying pressure, she sighed in relief.

Definitely, she could feel a little tenderness, but not enough to stop her progress. Soon, she would be riding on Bess, and after that, she'd be resting in her bed. By morning, no one would even notice she'd been out late.

First, she had to find the right spot to dig. The thick rope she would use to determine the distance from the tree to the treasure ought to be the correct length, since Grayson said he had measured and cut it in advance.

With the base of the tree as her starting point, Eleanor lay down the rope upon the ground. As the puzzle instructed, she made a beeline through the spot where the weight dropped, and onward for precisely fifty feet.

She, and the rope, ended up in a clearing, obviously thanks to Grayson's forethought. Not under a bush or in the middle of a tree.

Lightning flashed again, so bright, it was like a hundred oil lamps had been lit around her, and then the thunder shook the ground beneath her feet.

"Mercy!" she exclaimed, then ran back for the lantern and the shovel. Feeling, yet ignoring, the growing discomfort at her ankle, she was glad of the rope path, for she nearly lost her way.

As she begun to dig, she heard Bess whinnying in the distance. Poor horse, probably afraid of the storm.

When the next jagged streak of lightning hit the forest floor very close to her, she shrieked and would vow the hair on the back of her neck rose up.

Was it dangerous? She was relieved not to be high in the tree anymore, thinking that might have been the very next place the lightning struck. She barely had time to note the strong, earthy aroma of the storm before the heavens seemed to open up and pour upon her.

Drats! She ought to give up and go back to the fishing shelter. Except she simply could not. Giving up when so close was not a valid choice.

Grayson had done a good job of making the earth appear undisturbed. She had to use force to dig, the spade slicing into the packed dirt. However, he obviously hadn't wanted it to be too arduous, even though he would have been the one digging if they'd found the treasure together.

Unlike the bad luck of the fortune hunters in *The Gold Bug*, who had marked the ground under the right eye socket instead of the left and, thus, dug for hours before realizing their mistake, she had done it correctly the first time. In a very few minutes, the tip of her shovel connected with something.

"Success!" Eleanor yelled aloud. She removed another few spadefuls of dirt and then ruined her gloves completely scrabbling to extricate the treasure from the muddy ground. It felt like a jar, a simple kitchen jar which might hold practically anything.

Hm!

She could barely see for the rain in her eyes and then—*crack!*—she was momentarily blinded by lightning so close she could smell it.

Shrieking with terror—a terrible, delightful, exciting fear—she had to remind herself she wasn't safely tucked in her bed reading Mrs. Radcliffe. She was actually living it!

After the next thunderhead rumbled past, Eleanor considered whether she needed to recover the wagon or any of the supplies in it. She decided to leave it all except the lantern and the sealed jar, which she gripped tightly.

Beginning to make her way back to the shelter, she was glad the lightning had moved off to the west, already lighting up the sky in the distance. Under the deluge of rain, however, she started to limp, and the pain, which she had ignored in her excitement, seemed to increase in her left ankle with every step. She would be relieved to mount Bess and head back to Turvey House.

Holding the oil lamp out before her, she thought she'd gotten herself turned around by mistake. She started off in the other direction, but it was an impassable clump of briar bushes.

Frustrated, her leg throbbing, she spun about again, realizing she'd lost her way almost at once.

"Eleanor!" she admonished herself. "This is no time to be silly."

If there hadn't been thick black cloud cover, she could have seen the stars to guide herself, as she was adept at navigating by the stars. While looking up, hoping to determine her north from her south, she came abruptly to the edge of the riverbank.

As the bushes gave way to the dank, pungent aroma of the river, she couldn't contain a shriek of alarm. To her horror, she was teetering on the edge of a slippery muddy slope, lantern in one hand shining a glow upon the dark, raging waters and the precious glass jar in the other.

She couldn't even wave her arms to regain her balance for fear of losing either one of the prized items. Her boots were sliding forward. In a moment, she would be engulfed by the chilly blackness of the River Great Ouse, and no one would ever know what befell her.

And on her birthday, too!

CHAPTER EIGHTEEN

Gray saw Eleanor in front of him and his hair stood on end. She was falling, slowly, into the river, the toes of her boots were already in the water. But he was quicker. He had to be! If she perished, his life would also be over.

Swiftly setting down his lantern as he ran toward her, he grabbed for the back of her skirts, desperately fearful of knocking her farther down the shallow grade of the slope. Unfortunately, she dropped her lantern, and, with a splash, it disappeared beneath the rapids, all light extinguished.

At the same time, she screamed, a terrified, shrill sound, making him think they were both plunging to their deaths, until he realized they were still standing on the bank. Moreover, she was struggling *against* him.

"Eleanor! It is I."

"Gray?" She relaxed instantly, and he yanked her back and into his arms. "How can you be here?" she wondered.

"I could ask the same of you." And he would, when they were safe and dry.

"But I already know how *I* came to be here," she said. "But *you* are in London."

"Your teeth are chattering, and you're babbling. Let's get you home."

He'd dragged her away from the water's edge, and she hissed.

"What is it?" he asked. "Are you cold?"

"Yes," she agreed. "Keep going. Bess is at the fishing shelter, probably scared."

"Not half as scared as I was," Gray told her, trying to keep his tone calm but wanting to rage at her for her foolishness. "My horse is over there, not far."

She hissed again, and he slowed down. "Are you injured? Did you fall out of the tree?"

Eleanor remained silent.

"Tell me," he demanded.

"I did not fall," she said, her tone as supercilious as it could be given her wretched situation. "I jumped."

He swore long and loud. "Did you break something?"

"Absolutely not. A simple sprain to my ankle, I would say."

In a quick, easy movement, he swept her off her feet, making her shriek again.

"Next time, warn me," she said, sounding cross, but then she slipped an arm around his neck and settled against his chest.

He sighed with utter relief. If he'd lost her, two hearts would have gone into the river and perished. For as surely as he would hold onto her for the rest of their lives, she had captured his heart.

Rain dripping into his eyes, he was nearly back where he'd tethered Percy by the oak, when she asked, "How can you see where you're going?"

"Sheer determination," he muttered. "Actually, I've been out here in the dark so many times since I was a boy, I just know where I am."

She was shivering against him, and he decided it best to keep her talking.

"So, you found the treasure?"

"Yes." She was so quiet, it worried him. He jiggled her, to make her speak. "I'm holding the jar under my cloak," she added.

"I'm holding the real treasure," he told her. "Do you understand?"

He felt her nod, and nothing more. Luckily, they had found his horse. Setting Eleanor gently on her feet, he started to unbuckle his saddle.

"What are you doing?"

"We won't both fit with the saddle, and I don't think you're well enough to ride alone."

She hesitated, and then in a clear, strong voice, she said, "Nonsense. I'm perfectly able to ride a horse."

Was she? Focusing on staying in the saddle would probably keep her from drifting off to sleep as he sensed her body and brain wanted to do.

"That's my girl," he said, hoping she wasn't offended by the term.

She said nothing, merely limping closer to the horse.

"Just wait here," he ordered. "Lean against Percy while I find my lantern. It must have tipped over."

In a minute, he found it, and tripped. Snatching the lantern off the ground, he hoped he could relight it with the matches in his pocket, if they weren't damp. Luckily, they weren't.

Striking the head of the Lucifer match, he soon had the lamp emitting a cheery glow, like a giant firefly, the only light in the dark and cloudy landscape. He set it down by his horse.

Cupping his hands, he managed to get Eleanor high enough so she could toss her injured leg over the back of Percy and ride him astride, the full skirts of her habit pulled high up on her legs, with her cloak hanging down covering his horse's rear.

"You look the very image of a Gothic romantic heroine," he told her, grabbing the reins and the lamp before beginning the trek back to the lean-to.

"Thank you," she said. Then, "How did you find me? And why did you come back so late from Town?"

"As soon as Cam said he'd given you that damned book, I knew what you would do."

"Oh," she said, sounding chagrined. "I'm sorry."

After a long pause, she added, "When I read how Mr. Legrand and his friend found treasure, I knew you would have buried something for me to find. And it was my birthday, so I wanted to see what it was."

"Despite the fact that it was nighttime and stormy out?"

"When I left Turvey, it was neither," she pointed out.

"Cam is furious, and you've worried Margaret, which makes him more furious."

Another long pause, and then Eleanor said, "Perhaps we needn't say anything about the river. Bad enough I jumped out of the tree and sprained my ankle like a ninny."

"Bad enough," he agreed.

"You didn't answer why you returned."

"As you said, it's your birthday. I didn't intend to miss it. How could I know you would retire extraordinarily early and then go out like a madwoman into the elements?"

She said nothing.

"I'll tell you how I should have known," he said. "Because you are Eleanor Blackwood."

She laughed, and when she did, he knew everything was going to be all right.

Soon, he would have Bess under him, and they would be home well before midnight.

ELEANOR WISHED SHE COULD have simply tiptoed into Turvey House secretly the way she'd left. Yet, as soon as her brother-in-law either heard or spotted their horses, she heard his whoop of joy. Then a door slammed as he must have gone inside to tell Maggie.

Next came the mortifying, overly dramatic moment when Grayson insisted on carrying her inside after letting Jamie take the horses. The stable boy had glared at her ferociously. She had a feeling he'd gotten into trouble on her account, and she would make amends as best she could the next day.

Meanwhile, she had a fuming Earl of Cambrey to face and a pale-faced sister, who, if anything, looked even more beautiful for being worried.

"Eleanor!" Maggie cried as Grayson carried her, dripping wet and filthy, into the elegant drawing room. "What did you do? Just look at the state you're in. John, please ask Tilda for brandy for my sister. For all of us, actually. And warm milk. I don't know why, but I'm sure Eleanor needs warm milk."

"Yes, my sweet," he said, and disappeared from the drawing room momentarily.

Eleanor was glad, for his expression had been what she would describe as "provoked," and she was certain she was in for a tongue-lashing at his earliest convenience.

As soon as he came back, apparently, it was convenient, for he started in on her.

"I should never have given you a saddle," John said, standing over where she lay stretched out on the sofa.

"That wouldn't have stopped me," she confessed. "I would have taken one from the stables."

He put his hands on his hips. "Have you no remorse for nearly killing us with worry? Imagine how we felt when Gray came home and sent Maggie up to fetch you, only to find you had disappeared."

"Why did you send Maggie for me?" Eleanor asked Grayson, who stood at one end of the sofa, saying nothing.

"I was surprised you'd gone to your room so early, and I wanted to see you."

"Did you?" she repeated, feeling comforted all over, even before a glass of brandy was pressed into her hand by her brother-in-law, and her sister drew her sodden cloak out from behind her.

"Stop all this calm chit-chat," John ordered. "You are to be punished and confined to your room, and you should be tarred and feathered."

Eleanor couldn't help laughing, even as Maggie rolled her eyes.

"Why are you laughing?" the earl asked tersely, but Eleanor could hear the softening in his voice.

"Because I am not a child. I can go where I wish, when I wish, especially on my birthday."

His mouth gaped open. "Do you hear this?" John asked the room in general, his gaze swiveling from Grayson to Maggie.

Then Maggie laughed, too, stopping only when her husband frowned at her.

"You're right," she agreed. "This is serious."

Turning to Eleanor, she added, "And you should be sorry. Yes, you are an adult, but you didn't behave like one. You are dear to all of us, and that was extremely wrong of you to go out into the night alone."

Chastened by her sister's words, Eleanor was more than a little ashamed. She didn't like the annoyed expression the earl was still wearing, nor the disappointed look upon Grayson's face.

"I did behave like a child," she admitted. "And I am sorry for the worry I caused. I knew what I was doing was wrong, or I wouldn't have snuck out as I did."

"Scaring us all," John muttered, "especially poor Gray."

Eleanor glanced at him, and he nodded, looking quite somber.

"And I did get hurt," Eleanor said quietly, only because the throbbing in her ankle was becoming more painful, and she desperately wanted her boot off.

"Oh no!" Maggie exclaimed. "I assumed Gray was only carrying you as a romantic gesture."

ELEANOR

Eleanor shook her head and pointed. "My ankle, I twisted it."

Grayson crouched down at her feet and gave her riding boot a gentle tug.

"Ow!" she exclaimed. This was not going to be pleasant. "I fear my ankle is swollen."

"We should cut the boot off," Grayson said, looking to John, who muttered something about not being a butler as he left the room to get the necessary implement.

Eleanor sighed, relieved it was only her riding boots. "Fine. As long as they're not my Wellies."

Grayson smiled at her words, then he gave her a wink while they waited for Cam to find some shears.

"I'm sorry about your sofa," she told Maggie. "In my sodden state, I should have been put on the floor."

"Don't be silly. We were due to redecorate anyway. I was thinking peach and green colors."

"What!" John exclaimed, reentering the drawing room and looking even more distraught, probably fearing the expense once his wife started thinking of the latest styles for home decorating. He handed Grayson a pair of scissors from the cook.

"I'll have this off in a jiffy," he promised her. "Let me know if anything hurts while I cut."

In a couple minutes, with her boot in two pieces, her stockinged ankle was exposed to everyone's view.

"Not too bad," she said, feeling guilty for worrying everyone.

"The boot might have been stopping it from swelling any further," Grayson pointed out, "so don't be surprised if it gets bigger, but Cook should have some arnica, which will help." He looked pointedly at John again.

"I'm not a bloody errand boy," the earl said. "Where on earth is Cyril?" But he went out in search of arnica balm, nonetheless.

"Take her other boot off, too," Maggie instructed, "and we'll put her feet up high on a cushion. I know that helps with swelling."

"Let's stop fussing," Eleanor said, even as Grayson lifted her calf and then set it down upon a pillow. His touch on her leg caused shivers to course through her, and she took another sip of brandy.

When John returned, Maggie said, "Why don't you two gentlemen leave the room, and I'll spread some balm on my sister's ankle."

"Maybe a cigar would be in order," the earl suggested, "to celebrate your brave heroics." His tone held a note of mockery, even as he clapped Grayson on the back.

With her gaze fixed on the handsome man who had indeed been her hero that night, Eleanor caught the warm glance Grayson sent over his shoulder before he left.

When the door closed, Maggie raised Eleanor's hem and drew down her cream-colored stocking. "Do you love him?" she asked without preamble.

Eleanor blinked at Maggie. Then she recalled her sister's honesty years back when she had disclosed her love for John Angsley.

"Yes."

Maggie clapped her hands, and the gesture reminded Eleanor of herself. They smiled at each other.

"You approve, I take it," Eleanor said.

"He's a very fine man," Maggie said. "With dash-fire and good looks, too, don't you think?"

"I do, rather."

Maggie smoothed the balm on Eleanor's ankle. "It is rather plump along here." She trailed her fingers where the skin obviously had fluid under it. Then she closed the earthenware pot. "And does he return your affections?"

"I'm not entirely sure, but I believe he has feelings for me."

Covering Eleanor's legs once again with her skirts, Maggie yawned.

"You should have seen Gray earlier. He literally ran out of here upon learning of your disappearance, especially frantic when he found out Cam had given you the book. He definitely looked like a man with strong feelings, including panic, I must say."

Then she nodded at Eleanor's chest. "What have you been holding onto all this time?"

Eleanor had been clutching the muddy glass jar for so long, first in the storm and then on the horse, she'd forgotten it. Even with her wet, filthy gloves on, her hands were cold and her fingers a little stiff as she opened them to release the jar, which was stoppered with a cork. She let it rest on her stomach while she peeled off her gloves and placed them onto Maggie's outstretched hand. Then she picked it up again.

"It's the treasure," she whispered.

Maggie frowned. "You got caught in a storm and twisted your ankle for a jar?" She leaned forward, peering closely. "With a piece of paper in it?"

"Yes, but it was dark, and the jar was covered in dirt, so I couldn't really see what was inside."

"Well, shall we see what it says?" Maggie's lovely eyes sparkled with curiosity.

Eleanor had a feeling it was something special, and for her eyes alone. Before she could answer, suddenly, Grayson's voice came from the doorway.

"If you don't mind, Margaret, the message is for your sister only. Would you allow me a moment alone with her?"

Instead of taking offense at being asked to leave her own drawing room, Maggie looked positively elated. Beaming her signature dazzling smile, known to bring more than one suitor to his knees, she cocked her head at him.

"You must treat my sister with the care and respect she deserves, Grayson. As long as you do, you may have as many moments alone with her as you like."

She ran a cool hand over Eleanor's forehead and leaned in to kiss her.

"You're smudged with grime," Maggie whispered, "and he's still looking at you as if you were draped in silk and jewels at a ball. Strong feelings indeed!"

Eleanor raised a hand to her cheek.

"No, don't. You look adorable," Maggie added, before kissing one of her grubby cheeks.

Waggling a finger at Grayson as she passed him, the Countess of Cambrey silently left the room.

"What did she say?" he asked.

"That I'm dirty."

He laughed. "She didn't, did she?"

"Well, am I?"

He drew a handkerchief from his pocket and sat down on the edge of the sofa and wiped her forehead and cheeks. Lastly, he drew it across her nose, and then showed it to her.

She saw traces of muck and blanched.

"See," he said, "not too bad. I've already asked Tilda to draw a bath. I know how women sleep better when they've bathed."

Eleanor didn't care for what that implied, that he knew enough women at bedtime to have formed such an opinion.

"How was London?" she asked.

He shrugged. "I barely saw it. I was on a quest."

"Really? Then you didn't go there for entertainment?"

Grayson laughed, a sound she found so alluring, it sent a shiver along her spine and caused a flutter deep inside her.

"You are all the entertainment I could ever need or want," he told her.

The heat rose in her cheeks.

"Open the jar," he ordered.

CHAPTER NINETEEN

Swallowing, Eleanor tried to pull the cork out of the neck of the slender jar, but it wouldn't budge. Thinking quickly, she used her teeth, causing Grayson to laugh again, when the cork popped free.

"You are a wild miss!" he declared.

"That's what Beryl always says."

"She's right." He waited while she unrolled the piece of paper with trembling fingers.

Thankfully, she saw words. "If you'd written this in some mysterious invisible ink like the map, I might have had to do you bodily harm."

Still, he remained silent, so she glanced down and read:

Eleanor Blackwood, you are worth more than any pirate treasure. You have captured my whole heart, and I cannot live without you by my side, sharing life's grandest adventures together. Will you be my wife?
All my love, Grayson.

It was complimentary, but not flowery. It was romantic, but to the point. It was Grayson O'Connor precisely. She could no longer see the words for the tears coursing down her cheeks.

"That's good," he said, wiping her face again. "The tears help remove the grime."

And how easily he made her laugh, which she did then.

"Will you answer me, Miss Blackwood?"

She stared into his eyes, reaching up to move a lock of his black hair off his forehead where it covered his brow, when he captured her hand in his.

"I am honored," she told him. "Yes, I will be your wife. I love you. I have loved you, and I will love you always."

"We were supposed to be standing under the trees, in your favorite environment," he said. "But adventures have a way of taking twists and turns. And I had the opportunity to go to London and get you this."

Digging in his pocket, he drew out a box, and her heart, already pounding with all that was happening so quickly, sped up even more. He slid off a green silk ribbon and opened the small box for her. Nestled on black velvet was a gold ring with an oval-shaped emerald and four small diamonds around it.

"It's beautiful." Overwhelmed, her voice had come out as a whisper. "The green is exquisite."

"For my naturalist, Eleanor."

She laughed again, and then he slipped it onto her finger.

"It fits!" he said, sounding surprised.

"It does," she agreed, turning her hand this way and that. "Imagine what it will look like when the sun hits it. Or moonlight!"

She couldn't contain the squeal of excitement. Even with a throbbing ankle, this was the absolute best evening of her life.

"Do you think Maggie has any champagne? I do love bubbly wine."

Grayson grinned at her. "You're not childish at all. You're delightfully *childlike*. And I hope you always remain that way."

She shrugged, glad he appreciated her as she was, for she believed she was too old to change. "I think it's time you kissed me."

"Long past time," he said, leaning low and claiming her lips.

For the duration of his kiss, she no longer felt the pain in her ankle, no longer worried about being dirty on Maggie's sofa. She was Grayson's fiancée, and he was going to become her husband!

When he raised his head, she said, "I confess, I was worried when you so easily stopped . . . you know, what we were doing in the fishing shelter. Then when I found out you went to London, I didn't know what to think."

He put a finger to her lips.

"There was nothing easy about drawing away from you in the lean-to, silly woman. But I already knew I wanted you for my wife and that wasn't the way I wanted to treat you"

"You did know, didn't you? You wrote the note many days ago."

He nodded. "And I didn't want you finding it alone either and reading it without me beside you."

"True, it wouldn't have been the same sharing your proposal with Bess. But the entire Kidd adventure, start to finish, was a wonderful birthday gift."

"Now you know all my secrets," Grayson said.

Secrets! She wasn't going to start her engagement by withholding a secret from him, even if there were others that weren't hers to disclose.

Barely even hesitating, Eleanor made her confession. "I was teaching your mother to write. That's why I stayed at Angsley Hall. That's why I wouldn't come away with you when you left. I had promised her, and I don't break promises."

As long as he didn't ask her anything more about it!

His handsome brow crinkled into a frown. "Why on earth would she want to learn to write now?" Then he grinned. "But how wonderful. And you succeeded, in such a short time?"

Eleanor nodded. "Your mother is very smart."

He looked proud. "As soon as your ankle has healed, we'll go see her together and tell her our news."

"All right." She was interrupted from saying more as John and Maggie returned.

"There are only so many times we can stroll up and down our hallway," the earl pointed out.

"We didn't hear a thing," Maggie promised, although Eleanor would vow her sister already knew of her engagement, especially when the maid entered a moment later with champagne.

Sure enough, Maggie added, "Let me see your ring."

A WEEK AND A half later, they were on horseback going to see Mrs. O'Connor. During that time, Eleanor had finished her letters to her mother, to her oldest sister, Jenny, and to Beryl with the added surprising news of her engagement. Since they were not members of nobility, and since no one gave a fig, they decided on a short engagement of two months so they could get to the wedded bliss—and the marriage bed—as quickly as possible.

She'd also presented Grayson with her drawing of Percy, for which he vowed to build a frame and hang in their home as soon as she moved in. And she'd had the chance to sit with him under the stars on his captain's walk.

That evening, it seemed her life was unfolding before her, just like the night sky twinkling above, endless and filled with wonder.

Yet, Eleanor couldn't shake the pangs of anxiety when she imagined the upcoming visit to Angsley Hall. They would visit with his mother first, and then go see Lord and Lady Angsley.

After putting their horses in the stable, they walked hand-in-hand toward the old granary lodge. Mrs. O'Connor spied them immediately as she was outside hanging her washing on a clothesline stretched between two straight birch trees. She hugged each of them in turn, and then Grayson told her their news.

After his mother exclaimed with joy, Eleanor showed her the ring, and then they had to have another round of hugging.

"Come in for tea," Mrs. O'Connor invited. "I'm so excited to be having a daughter at last."

It seemed to Eleanor as if no time had passed since she'd first been yanked into Mrs. O'Connor's home, mistaken for Phoebe. On the other hand, she felt years older. And there was now a special bond between her and this woman whose son she loved beyond anything.

Unfortunately, the knot of unease wouldn't release, not while Eleanor knew there was a huge secret between mother and son.

Casually, as the tea steeped in the blue pot covered in a knitted tea cozy to keep it hot, Grayson said, "Eleanor told me she taught you to read."

Mrs. O'Connor's gaze flew to hers, and she smiled reassuringly at the older woman.

"I didn't want any secrets between Grayson and me, and I needed him to know why I'd stayed behind."

His mother nodded, realizing Eleanor had said nothing more.

"What are you planning to write?" he asked, sounding genuinely interested.

His mother hesitated, and Eleanor held her breath.

"A letter," Mrs. O'Connor said finally.

"To whom?" he asked, and Eleanor wished he would leave his mother alone.

Mrs. O'Connor turned to face her son fully. "I plan to write a letter to someone I love with all my heart. I told your wonderful young lady how it would mean the world to me if I could do so."

He stared at his mother. Eleanor could see he was thinking. If she were in his shoes, she might first wonder if his mother wanted to write to an old flame. But then, knowing how Mrs. O'Connor doted on him, he should realize the letter was to him.

After a pause, he said, "Eleanor and I would be pleased if you would come live with us. There is plenty of room. And when we have children, it would be...," his words struggled to a halt, for Mrs. O'Connor was already shaking her head.

"I cannot. I can never live at Turvey House or on its property."

Another long pause ensued.

Eleanor wished she understood. She and Grayson had discussed it and hoped the lure of grandchildren would bring his mother away from the granary lodge.

"Are you in love with Mr. Stanley?" Grayson asked.

Eleanor gasped right along with Mrs. O'Connor.

The woman's hand flew first to her throat and then to cover her mouth. She shook her head as if to say no, but when her words came out, they were in the affirmative.

"I am. He is a sweet and caring man."

Grayson covered his mother's hand. "I'm happy for you. Truly."

Eleanor assumed their love was not new, but it was neither her nor Grayson's place to probe further.

"Do you have an understanding?" he asked.

This time, his mother smiled. "We do. When he retires, not too long from now, he will be given three acres and a house. We shall marry or maybe just have a simple handfasting. It matters not. We shall live out our days together."

Grayson nodded. After the briefest hesitation, he asked, "Is he my father?"

"What? No!" his mother said at once. "If your father were Mr. Stanley, why wouldn't I have told you?"

"I don't know. Perhaps to give me a better life than if I were the bastard child of a butler. Without a known father, I've been able to move easily between the world of servants and the Angsleys. For my whole life that I can remember, I've been the best friend of a man who inherited the earldom. Cam treats me like a brother. You made that possible by keeping my father a secret."

When his mother pursed her lips tightly, he shook his head.

"It's no matter. Now I know the reason you wouldn't come live with me, even after you retired. You have your Mr. Stanley, and I'm happy for you."

However, Mrs. O'Connor didn't look happy, not one bit. She rose to her feet and silently went into her bedroom.

Eleanor exchanged a questioning look with Grayson.

"Do you think she's all right?" she asked.

"Maybe you should go in there," he said, looking uncomfortable. "I don't know what I said wrong."

Just then, his mother returned, her face pale, and Eleanor thought it was with fear, not anger. She looked terrified, but her first words gave nothing away.

"Eleanor, dear girl," Mrs. O'Connor began, and she was positive Grayson's mother was going to ask her to leave. "I want to thank you again for teaching me to write. And I shall use what you've given me. I might make up a poem or write down my recipes. Wouldn't it have been nice if old Cook had done that before she passed?"

She was talking quickly, clearly not expecting an answer. "And now, I can read, too. Those primers were easy, and I returned them to Nanny Wendall. I've borrowed a book by Ellis Bell, *Wuthering Heights*, and I don't even know what the title means, but I'm muddling through it. Frankly, it's a bit dour."

Grayson and Eleanor remained silent. They knew his mother wasn't really wanting to have a discussion of literature at that moment. She had something else on her mind.

She leaned a hand on the table, staring at her son.

"Grayson, I haven't told you the truth. Now you're marrying, I know I did wrong keeping it from you. I don't think it will make a difference, but you have a right to know. I was going to put it in a letter for after I'm gone."

"Mum!"

"I know. That was being cowardly. Eleanor tried to tell me."

He turned to her, his eyes questioning. "Do you know what this is about?"

How hurt he would be if she had known! She'd never been happier than that moment to be completely ignorant of something. "I do not. I promise."

"Of course not," his mother said. "Listen, for I must get this out before I lose my nerve. I did something stupid when I was a lass, but I have no regrets because I have you."

He nodded. "Then I *am* a bastard?"

"Yes," she said softly.

Eleanor watched this unfolding, ready to jump in and assure him it made no difference to her desire to marry him, not a whit!

"And the reason I can never live on the Cambrey estate is because," Mrs. O'Connor hiccupped, and Eleanor realized the woman was beginning to cry, "because I promised your father I wouldn't."

With that, she opened the hand she had fisted on the table and a gold ring rolled off her palm toward Grayson.

He stared at it a moment before picking it up. Eleanor could see it was a signet ring, small enough for a man's little finger, where it would rest, ready for sealing documents whenever necessary.

"It was a mistake," Grayson's mother continued. "I believed I loved him, but, for him, I was a momentary madness. He truly loved his wife until the day he died, and I had vowed to him never to bring her a bit of grief."

ELEANOR

Abruptly, Grayson stood up. "Does Cam know?"

Eleanor was trying to follow what was happening, but they had lost her.

"No. No one outside of this room. Your father took it to his grave."

Grayson slammed the ring onto the table, making all the cups and saucers jump, as well as the teapot and Eleanor. Then he turned, yanked open the door, and stalked out.

CHAPTER TWENTY

"Gray," Eleanor called after him. Then she turned to Mrs. O'Connor, her future mother-in-law, who had tears streaming down her face.

"I don't understand. Please tell me. What does it mean? Who is his father?"

"Look at the ring, dear."

Eleanor picked it up, studying the plain gold ring with a *G* and a *C* cast into the flat surface.

Their conversation came clear. "Gideon Cambrey," she surmised, thinking of what this meant. "John wears one just like it."

"This is the original," Grayson's mother said. "The old earl—he wasn't old, then, mind you, nor even that old when he died, poor man—he never wanted to hurt his wife, but he also wanted me to be able to prove my claim someday, at least to Gray. The earl made himself a new ring after he gave this one to me. But the *G* isn't for Gideon. It's for Godridius de Chambrai, a knight of William the Conqueror."

"William the Conqueror," Eleanor couldn't help echoing, thinking of a family line that stretched so far back in history.

"The current earl, your sister's husband, can tell you all about that. Every signet ring made for their family has always been the same."

Eleanor considered a moment. "John and Grayson already love each other like brothers. And the Angsleys...," she trailed off.

"They've always treated him like family." His mother drew a handkerchief from her pocket and wiped her face.

"But they didn't know?" Eleanor asked.

Mrs. O'Connor shook her head. "No. They all like Gray for his own sake. I hope that will be the saving grace." She started to cry again. "Go find him. Make sure he's all right. Ask him not to hate me."

Eleanor surged to her feet and embraced Mrs. O'Connor. "No, of course he doesn't. He is just stunned. I'll bring him back."

And setting the ring upon the table, she chased after her fiancé.

GRAY WANTED TO HOWL. This changed everything—who he was, how he fit in, why Gideon Cambrey had been so kind to him for all those years. The old earl was his father!

"Arrrr," he yelled, long and loud, staring at the rich blue sky.

Today, of all days, it was a perfect autumn display with a brilliant gilded sun, without a single cloud, and not a drop of water raining down upon him. And yet he felt as though he were drowning.

He knew Eleanor would find him, even if he hadn't yelled. In a few minutes, he turned from where he was leaning against the railing, stroking Percy's neck, and there she was.

She looked uncertain, which twisted his gut.

"Are you all right?" she asked, approaching closer.

"I don't know." *Was that his voice, so gruff and strange?*

"Tell me what you are thinking. What is the worst of this? And then I'll remind you of the best."

"I'm thinking I am not the man I thought I was."

"You are." She stood right beside him, setting her dainty foot, now healed, onto the first railing and then stepping up so their heads were at equal height.

"You're Grayson O'Connor, fruit of your mother's womb. A capable man, an estate manager, loved by many, including me." She leaned her shoulder against his. "And admired by all."

He couldn't wrap it up into such a neat package. At least, not yet.

"Cam—John—is my half-brother! Our father cheated on Cam's mother with *my* mother. If he knew, that alone would hurt him. He revered his father."

He fell silent a moment, then shook his head. "John Angsley is truly my blood brother, yet I cannot tell him. For then, he would have to keep this secret from his mother. And that would gut him."

He groaned. "How will I look Lady Cambrey in the eyes when she returns from London?"

"As you always have," Eleanor assured him. "Look at her as a dear woman who has treated you with kindness and who took you into her home when you were a little boy, to be companion to her only surviving child."

He considered that. "I'm glad she doesn't know. She is a gracious lady, and she might have viewed me differently had she known I was her husband's bastard. I'm glad he's dead," he finished, knowing he spoke harshly.

She lay her hand upon his arm. "I never knew him, but I have always understood Gideon Angsley to have been a kind and smart man. However, no one ever said he was infallible."

He looked at her, captivated by her soft brown eyes.

"I cannot begrudge him his infidelity," she added, "for I cannot bear the idea of you not existing. And I would wager everyone who knows you would feel the same way, particularly John."

He sighed, the best he could do in lieu of a smile.

Eleanor reached her hand to the back of his neck, tugging at him to lean closer. When he did, she kissed him, full on the mouth, in front of Percy and any stable boy who might be watching. She even nibbled on his lower lip as she drew away.

"Does that feel any different?"

"No," he said begrudgingly.

"Are we still getting married?" she asked.

"I'm a bastard," he pointed out.

She shrugged. "I'm happy to be Mrs. O'Connor. If I were another Angsley wife, like my sister, it would only confuse matters."

He smiled. *How could she make light of such an important matter?* Yet, with a few words, she had lessened the tension inside him.

"Would you love the Angsleys or Beryl and her siblings or John any differently or any more if you had known?" she asked, leaning her head against his shoulder.

He pondered her question. He'd always thought of them as family, and without knowing the truth, treated his cousins as his cousins and Cam as his brother.

"No," he agreed. "In my heart, everything is the same. Except now I know who my father was and what he was like, instead of him being a mysterious man from the distant past who never knew me."

"And the earl made sure to have you close so you would, indeed, know him," she pointed out.

Unexpectedly, tears pricked his eyes.

Dammit! He was going to cry if he wasn't careful.

"Your mother is worried you hate her."

"Dear God! Of course not. She did everything for me, including giving me up to be raised by the man who didn't love her and by the wife whom he adored."

"That must have been hard for her," Eleanor agreed, refusing to let him wallow.

"I know." Then he recalled the *proof*. "But that ring must stay with her. If it ever was found with us at Turvey House, it would hurt people."

She nodded her agreement, then cocked her head at him in a way he found utterly enticing. As usual, when he looked at her sweet, upturned mouth, he had to force himself to listen to her words and not merely watch her lips.

"Although there may come a time," Eleanor pointed out, as they began to walk back to his mother's lodging, "when our sons and daughters are older, you may want to tell them who their grandfather was. And by then, it might not hurt anyone. Maybe then, you will claim your ring."

Grayson drew her arm through his. Up ahead, his mother was standing by her front door, waiting. He waved to her to signal all was well.

"Miss Blackwood, how did a woman of such tender years as yourself become so wise?"

She gave a long sigh. "Mr. O'Connor, I attribute it to many hours of reading Gothic novels."

EPILOGUE

"Eleanor!" came Grayson's voice, loudly and urgently. "Where are you?"

Lightning split the sky in the distance and sizzled the air. She laughed. This was the best place to be in the whole world as she watched the storm clouds roll in.

The hatch to the captain's walk suddenly snapped open, making Eleanor gasp. Then Grayson's head appeared, followed by the rest of him.

"I'm here!" she said belatedly, jumping up from where she'd been seated on the roof of their home while peering through the telescope.

"Didn't you see me arrive?" he asked, taking her in his arms.

"I confess, I was not looking for you but at the sky. The stars were out only minutes ago, and then—" She gestured to the horizon and the massive thunderheads. "All that blew in. Isn't it wonderful?"

"I looked for you in the drawing room and our bedroom. But naturally, since a vicious storm is about to strike, my delightful wife is on the rooftop."

She giggled, grabbed his face between her hands, and kissed him. When she released him, she asked, "Did you solve the problem?"

Grayson had been called to the main house when the upstairs plumbing was gurgling in the bathtub, just as Maggie's nanny was trying to bathe Rosie.

Maggie, ready to deliver any day, could not possibly bend down to bathe her daughter which she loved to do, making her already a little cranky. Everyone wanted to keep her happy and calm, even if that meant plumbing work at nighttime

"I did. Rosie had stuffed her cloth bunny in the drain. Everything is fine now, and when I left, Margaret had her feet in the air to lessen the swelling in her ankles, declaring the baby inside her wanted strawberries and sponge cake. I stayed with Cam for a little while and had a glass of brandy while poor Cook started baking. It's mayhem, frankly."

"It will all return to normal after the baby is born," Eleanor mused as thunder boomed in the distance.

Loud and insistent barking drew her attention to their own small charges.

"I guess the dogs know the storm is nearly upon us." They'd taken all four of Lord Angsley's hunting spaniels a month earlier since he rarely hunted anymore, too busy as the queen's ambassador to Spain, and the dogs were neglected and restless. Eleanor enjoyed walking with them twice a day in any weather and turning them into well-trained pets.

"Let's go downstairs before they start chewing up the chair legs again," Grayson suggested.

She laughed. Apparently, he had noticed their dogs weren't quite so well-trained yet.

Her husband descended the compact circular staircase ahead of her to the landing at the end of their upstairs hallway. Then he turned to make sure she came down safely.

Silly, sweet, dear man! It was simply a staircase, albeit narrow and winding, but his chivalrous manner of caring for her touched her heart as much as ever.

It had been five months since their country wedding at St. Paul's Church in Bedford. Five months of evenings spent learning about each other, laughing, stumping each other with ever more difficult riddles, and reading together in the drawing room.

Five months of love and lovemaking, of learning what it meant to be a husband and wife, and enjoying every minute of it.

Mrs. O'Connor had even come to their home for the first time, although she still vowed never to set foot in Turvey House. She and Mr. Stanley would be setting up their own home in the upcoming summer, when the butler retired.

Holding hands, Grayson and Eleanor went downstairs. Barking seemed to be coming from everywhere at once, so they spent a few minutes herding the spaniels into the drawing room and settling them on the rug with a bone each.

Grayson poured himself a brandy and Eleanor, a glass of sherry, which she preferred. They ran a small household, with a part-time cook for evening meals, and only two maids to help out. She adored everything about her life, especially their evenings.

Their drawing room was more like a library. Naturally, after marriage, she brought her books to nestle on the shelves with those Grayson already had. Moreover, her family had given them volumes as wedding presents, including a Shakespeare collection from her Scottish cousin Maisie and some pirate stories from Beryl and Philip. More books seemed to arrive weekly.

Nearly every night, they read together, often aloud, sharing stories or silently seated side by side, each with their own interest. Tonight, Eleanor had a surprise for her husband, a secret she'd been keeping for a month.

"May I read you something tonight?" she asked him when he sat down on the sofa next to her.

"I am nearly at the end of *The Last of the Mohicans*. It's rather gripping," he said, and she feared he might turn her down. "But I would rather listen to you read Cook's shopping list simply for the pleasure of hearing your voice."

Shaking her head at his obscene flattery, Eleanor rose once more and went to the shelf where she'd left a leather sheath filled with paper. Then she resumed her place beside him.

"What is this?" he asked, leaning close.

Just then, lightning flared outside their paned windows and thunder rocked their house, sending shivers down her spine and causing the dogs to start nervously barking again.

She hugged the pages to her chest. "Sit back," she ordered her husband, waiting until he had done so. "Quiet!" she commanded the spaniels, who miraculously obeyed.

"I shall read you the title—*The Widow's Walk*."

"Never heard of it," Grayson said. "Who wrote it?"

Taking a deep breath, she looked up, her gaze locking with his. "Edgar Blackwood."

He frowned, and then, slowly, a smile spread upon his face. "You are looking particularly lovely tonight, Edgar."

She giggled, feeling nervous at sharing her work-in-progress.

"It's a Gothic novel," she confessed. "With the title being a play on words of our roof walk as well as meaning some creepy widows walking. People will have to read it to find out. Of course, most of the women are dressed all in black and are rather a scary crew. And our heroine, Isabella, is hoping not to become one of them by saving her husband who is incarcerated for piracy and who might hang. If she can locate the true pirate's treasure, she will have proof of his innocence."

"That's wonderful," he enthused. "*You* are wonderful."

"I haven't figured it all out yet. I only had the germ of an idea about a month ago. This is just the first few chapters."

"You have the patience and intelligence and love of story to be an excellent writer. I have no doubt. And you can even illustrate your own book."

She shrugged. "I hadn't considered that far ahead. I simply thought since I have now lived a Gothic adventure, thanks to you, I could write one, too. Or maybe a few of them. I seem to be filled with ideas."

He leaned close again and whispered against her ear, "I want to kiss you and then take you upstairs early."

His confession left her momentarily speechless, while anticipation trickled through her. When his lips touched the skin at her neck, she tingled all over, and her breath escaped in a sigh of pleasure.

"In fact, I want to make ardent love to you, Edgar," Grayson added, and Eleanor began to laugh until tears came to her eyes.

After she'd gathered herself, he said, "But first, dear wife, read to me."

He leaned his head back against the sofa, folded his hands in his lap, and closed his eyes. "Read me your story."

ABOUT THE AUTHOR

USA Today bestselling author Sydney Jane Baily writes historical romance set in Victorian England, late 19th-century America, the Middle Ages, the Georgian era, and the Regency period. She believes in happily-ever-after stories for an already-challenging world with engaging characters and attention to period detail.

Born and raised in California, she has traveled the world, spending a lot of exceedingly happy time in the U.K. where her extended family resides, eating fish and chips, drinking shandies, and snacking on Maltesers and Cadbury bars. Sydney currently lives in New England with her family—human, canine, and feline.

You can learn more about her books and contact her via her website at SydneyJaneBaily.com.

Made in the USA
Monee, IL
30 August 2021